# THE LOTTERY

Skye Fargo was just falling asleep on his bedroll under the star-filled sky when he heard a faint sound. He sat up and reached for his gun. Then he heard the half-whispered call: "Fargo?"

"Over here," he said, and a form appeared, took shape.

"Chrissie," he frowned. "What the hell are you doing here?"

The sixteen-year-old girl wore a flimsy nightdress. She also wore an excited smile. "I won," she said, kneeling beside him.

"You won what?"

"I get to come to you first. I drew the longest straw."

"You drew straws?" said Skye, still unbelieving. "All of you?"

"All of us," said Chrissie, and slowly she drew her nightdress up over her long, lithe, high-breasted body, then impatiently tossed it aside. . . .

# SIGNET Westerns You'll Enjoy

# THE TRAILSMAN 6

# DAKOTA WILD

by

## Jon Sharpe

A SIGNET BOOK

**NEW AMERICAN LIBRARY**

TIMES MIRROR

## PUBLISHER'S NOTE

This novel is a work of fiction. Names, characters, places and incidents are either the product of the author's imagination or are used fictitiously, and any resemblance to actual persons, living or dead, events, or locales is entirely coincidental.

NAL BOOKS ARE AVAILABLE AT QUANTITY DISCOUNTS WHEN USED TO PROMOTE PRODUCTS OR SERVICES. FOR INFORMATION PLEASE WRITE TO PREMIUM MARKETING DIVISION, THE NEW AMERICAN LIBRARY, INC., 1633 BROADWAY, NEW YORK, NEW YORK 10019.

The first chapter of this book appeared in *The River Raiders*, the fifth volume of this series.

SIGNET TRADEMARK REG. U.S. PAT. OFF. AND FOREIGN COUNTRIES REGISTERED TRADEMARK—MARCA REGISTRADA HECHO EN CHICAGO, U.S.A.

SIGNET, SIGNET CLASSICS, MENTOR, PLUME, MERIDIAN and NAL BOOKS are published by The New American Library, Inc., 1633 Broadway, New York, New York 10019

First Printing, May, 1981

1 2 3 4 5 6 7 8 9

PRINTED IN THE UNITED STATES OF AMERICA

# The Trailsman

Beginnings . . . they bend the tree and they
mark the man. Skye Fargo was born when he was
eighteen. Terror was his midwife, vengeance his
first cry. Killing spawned Skye Fargo, ruthless,
cold-blooded murder. Out of the acrid smoke of
gunpowder still hanging in the air, he rose, cried
out a promise never forgotten.

The Trailsman, they began to call him, all
across the West: searcher, scout, hunter, the
man who could see where others only looked,
his skills for hire but not his soul, the man who
lived each day to the fullest, yet trailed each
tomorrow. Skye Fargo, the Trailsman, the seeker
who could take the wildness of a land and the
wanting of a woman and make them his own.

*The town of Moosehead, Wisconsin,*
*bordering the Dakota Territory—1861.*

# 1

"I obviously have the wrong room," the young woman said, looking at him with disdain and icy disapproval. "I'm looking for a Mr. Fargo," she said.

Skye Fargo blinked, drew his lips back, ran his tongue over his teeth, blinked again. His eyes hurt and he knew they were red. His mouth felt like he'd been chewing on a bale of cotton, his head seemed to be splitting in two and her knock on the door had sounded like a thousand sledgehammers. "Come in, goddammit," he had called to stop the pounding, sat up in the wrinkled bed, and now she stood there, one hand on the doorknob, her eyes holding onto the magnificence of his naked torso, the hard-muscled body.

"I'm sorry to have disturbed you," she said with cold disapproval. "Perhaps he's in the next room." She started to back out, pull the door closed.

"I'm Fargo," he growled, squinted up at her. She was good-looking under that icy stare, with dark-blue eyes, a thin, delicate nose, nice, sharp-lined lips, a high bustline under a dark-gray high-necked dress with a neat pink collar.

"You are Mr. Fargo?" She frowned back.

"You got a hearing problem?" he growled, swung long, powerful legs over the edge of the bed. The wrinkled sheet fell away from his groin.

1

"Please!" he heard her cry sharply, saw her look away at once.

"Shit," he muttered, noticing he had a half-erection, and pulling the sheet back over his equipment.

She looked back at him disdainfully. "You're drunk." She sniffed. The room did smell like a used still, he admitted silently.

"Wrong. I *was* drunk. I might get drunk again. But I'm not drunk now," he said, tried to remember how many shots of bourbon he'd put away last night. Too many, that was for damn sure, he reckoned, squinted up at the young woman. "Who the hell are you?" he rasped.

"I'm Karen Fisher," she said stiffly. "But that's of no matter, now. I may have the right person but I've obviously made a mistake."

"How'd you track me here?" Fargo frowned, tried to lick the dryness from his lips.

"A Mr. William Davis suggested I come see you," she said.

"Willie," Fargo grunted, swore under his breath. Willie knew what he'd been doing last night. "Remind me to break Willie's skull," he muttered to the girl.

"I shall do nothing of the kind, but I do intend to give Mr. Davis a piece of my mind for sending me to a man of your type," Karen Fisher said severely.

"What type is that?" Fargo glared back at her.

Karen Fisher looked down her lovely, thin nose at him. "A drunkard," she snapped. "Any man in your condition at this hour of the morning is obviously a drunkard."

"Any man in my condition at this hour of the morning has had a fucking good time," he said.

Karen Fisher's lips pressed tight. "I'll definitely have a word with Mr. Davis," she snapped as she spun around.

"Tell him not to send me any more prunes for breakfast," Fargo called after her.

She glared back. "Lout," she snapped, and slammed the door.

"Bitch," he yelled as his head seemed to explode. He lay back on the wrinkled sheets again and wondered when the girl had left last night. He remembered only that she'd been young and new at being a dance-hall girl and that made her a good companion for the night. Six weeks on a hard trail up from Abilene and he'd been ready for a wild night of unwinding. He'd had it and then some from the way he felt. He pulled himself up, plunged his head into the deep basin of cold water that stood in a corner of the hotel room, did it twice more, and dried himself with a coarse towel. Slowly, he began to feel himself, did a dozen deep knee bends, and began to dress. Before going out for the night, he'd posted his paycheck back to a bank he used in Kentucky, a habit he'd taught himself years back.

Besides, Moosehead was a hard town, a place of people on the move, heading out to the badlands, some of them, others nursing a dream of a home in the wilderness, some trying for the long haul to the West Coast, and still others struggling back, defeat and despair their only baggage. A town like that held a lot of drifters looking for the easy mark and the fast buck. Fargo strapped his gun belt on, adjusted the hang of the holster with the big Colt .45, and stepped from the room. He left the door ajar for the room to air out some, went down the hall to the seedy lobby and outside. His head had almost stopped hurting him and he strolled to Willie Davis' general store. Willie, a genial, round-faced man with short-cropped brown hair, saw him coming and stepped from behind the counter, held both palms upward.

"Now, easy, Fargo. I didn't think she was going to go find you right away," Willie said.

"I don't know if I ought to believe you, Willie," the big black-haired man said. "You'd just get a damn kick out of doing that."

3

Willie Davis grinned. "I would, but I didn't do it this time," he said.

Fargo let his lake-blue eyes soften, found a little smile, and eased down against the counter of the cluttered store. "Who the hell was she, anyway?" he asked.

"She came in here asking me if I knew anybody that could lead her and a wagonload of young boys from some military academy into the Dakota Territory, up to Beulah."

"A wagonload of young boys into the Dakota Territory? She loco?" Fargo frowned.

Willie Davis shrugged. "Maybe, damn determined, though. I told her the trailsman, the very best there was, happened to be in town and she could find you at the hotel."

"She found me, wasn't too happy about it, though," Fargo said.

"I know. She came back here steaming mad, said she couldn't have a damn drunkard leading a wagonload of young boys on a long trip. I tried to tell her you weren't really a drunk." Willie grinned.

"Thanks," Fargo muttered.

"She said you were real unfriendly, *ungracious* was the word she used," Willie said, grinning again.

"She woke me out of a sleep I sure needed," Fargo said. "Where'd she haul in from?"

"Don't know. Never saw her before. She bought supplies, mostly food and some extra tarpaulins, six, in fact," Willie said.

"Six extra tarpaulins? What the hell for?" Fargo wondered aloud.

"Search me. She's not the kind you question."

"I know, real snooty," Fargo muttered.

"You want to see her about the job, she and her boys are staying in the old Kenner cabin at the end of town," the storekeeper said.

4

"No, thank you," Fargo said. "She may be loco. I'm not." He picked up a cotton shirt. "I'll take this so's you remember me till next time I come this way, Willie."

"Where you going now, Fargo?" the other man asked.

"I'm going to ride the edge of the Dakota Territory for a few days, it just so happens, up to Sioux Falls. Word's come to me that somebody I'm looking for might be there," Fargo said, and the lake-blue eyes suddenly became blue shale.

"One of the three?" Willie asked quickly, and the big black-haired man nodded, his face as if carved in stone. Fargo's thoughts flashed back to that day, too many years back and still clear as yesterday, when the three rotten plotters had slain his ma and pa and kid brother. Skye Fargo had been born that day, out of the stench of death, and no matter what trails he took, that one remained etched inside him. Someday, someplace, he'd find them, together or one at a time. He'd stopped counting how many false leads he'd chased. Yet he'd continue to track down each of them. Someday, one would be right.

"Luck to you, Fargo," Willie said, and Fargo's thoughts came back to the moment.

"Keep selling your leaky pots and pans to the poor farmers who come by here, Willie," Fargo said, strode from the store. Moosehead was busy with a parade of wagons and horsemen, big heavy flatbed drays and Conestogas, some stake-sided wagons fitted out with canvas. He made his way through the crowded, churned-up mud of Main Street, halted at the dance hall as the girl called to him from the doorway. He stepped inside, the place dim and dreary even in the light of day.

"See you tonight?" she asked, and he looked at her. She was still young, but her prettiness had seemed more so when observed through bourbon, her legs thinner, her breasts under the loose open top of the dress flatter.

5

"Can't say," he told her, and she hooked her arm in his, her face growing serious.

"On me, tonight," she said. "You're something special."

He patted her rear, accepted the compliment given in the only way he knew how, wished he could remember her name. He walked on to the stable and the old man came out of the rear with the pinto at once. "I make a living remembering men and their horses, but it'd be pretty hard not to remember this one," he said, looking with admiration at the Ovaro pinto, jet-black forequarters and hindquarters, gleaming white in between. Fargo took the horse, paid the stableman, and swung into the saddle. He wouldn't be staying the night in Moosehead. One wild night was enough, one night under a roof more than sufficient. Too many people too close together in town. He headed for the lonely beauty of the land. At the end of town he passed the old Kenner cabin. It was empty, the door left hanging open. Karen Fisher and her wagon of young boys had left.

He shook his head and rode on, crossing into the Dakota Territory as the day started to slip to a close. He rode up along the border where wagon tracks turned inland, followed until dark settled in. He found a stand of thick oak, spread his bedroll, and slept soundly until the dawn sun woke him. He washed in a nearby stream, leisurely breakfasted on some johnnycakes, and rode on. The Dakota Territory quickly turned into rolling grasslands with higher ridges that formed a pattern of high and low areas. He'd ridden through the morning and into the early afternoon when he halted on one of the ridges. Below, two Conestoga wagons moved, one behind the other. He watched, moved the pinto down from the top of the ridge and into a thin line of pin cherry that let him draw closer and stay out of sight.

Karen Fisher, in leather skirt and high-buttoned white blouse, drove the first wagon. Two young boys in the uniform of the private military academy rode the driver's seat of the second wagon, wearing high-collared blue jackets, gray trousers, high-buttoned shoes, and high caps that fitted close to the head with short peaks. Fargo glimpsed others inside the Conestoga as it moved on, all in the same uniform. He watched the wagons roll on, but he stayed behind the trees. His eyes flicked to the distant ridge on the opposite side where the tiny spiral of dust rose into the air. Moving slowly with it, staying in the line of pin cherries, he waited, watched, saw the spiral become four riders as they crested the distant ridge. His eyes narrowed as he watched. They were following the two Conestogas and he let them disappear down the other side of the ridge, spurred the pinto on.

He turned, crossed over to another ridge, but stayed off the top, letting his eyes move from the four riders to the wagons and back again. It wasn't likely that Karen Fisher knew she was being followed, he decided. She drove the lead Conestoga into a cluster of oak and halted as the dusk deepened. Fargo watched as the second wagon drew up near the first and a dozen or so lithe, uniformed figures clambered from it. His eyes moved across the ground to where the distant ridge rose opposite him, saw that the tiny spiral of dust had vanished. The four riders had also halted someplace on the far ridge and he returned his glance to the distant Conestogas. He frowned as he saw the uniformed figures string up a series of ropes, from the wagon frames to the trees. The six tarpaulins were brought out and hung over the ropes to enclose the area. He saw one of the boys adjusting the tarpaulins, sealing the area from prying eyes with the canvas fence.

Karen Fisher had a big thing about privacy or she thought the tarpaulins made the enclosure safe, he murmured to himself as he moved the pinto closer. In a little while, he saw a dim flicker behind the tarpaulins. They'd built a fire inside their fence, visible from close by only.

7

Maybe she did figure the tarpaulins as a safety measure, he reckoned, as he brought the pinto to the very edge of the trees and halted. He dismounted as darkness settled over the scene. Curiosity more than anything else made him sit down, make himself comfortable. It was just possible that the four riders were moving along in the same direction as the Conestogas and really not following them at all. Possible, he pondered, but not likely. They'd kept too steady a pace, hanging back when four horsemen moving on their own would have caught up to the two wagons.

He lay down on his stomach, took the big Colt out, and put it on the ground before him. Using his arm as a pillow, he leaned his head down and catnapped. The four riders, if they came down from the other ridge, would have to cross in front of him. He had the hearing of an Indian, attuned to the sounds of the wild, perhaps a gift of his one-quarter-Cherokee heritage. He'd hear them if he were napping, the step of a horse's hoof, the faint creak of saddle leather, or see them if he were awake.

He closed his eyes, napped, and in between, continued to wonder what in hell made a young woman think she could squire a wagonload of boys through the untamed Dakota Territory and get through alive. The four riders could be explained a lot easier. He was dozing when the first gray light of day slid over the ridges; he woke instantly, but not because of the dim light. The faint sound of metal touched his ears, a spur brushing against a stirrup, and he snapped awake, lay unmoving, another lesson he had learned long years back. Like a creature of the forest, he'd learned that sudden movement could bring swift death.

He peered over his arm, saw the four horsemen approach the tarpaulin-hung enclosure, spread out, and begin to dismount. Drifters, he figured, worn clothing and worn gun belts, that stray-dog look about them. The nearest one moved with silent but tentative motions, a long, drawn face under a battered flat-brimmed hat. He motioned to the others and they began to approach the wagons on foot. He halted at the nearest tarpaulin, pushed one edge aside to peer into the enclosure, satisfied there was nothing inside it, and started to climb into the wagon. Fargo rose, waited till he was inside, moved forward, heard the brief, muffled cry from the Conestoga, Karen Fisher's voice. The other three were starting to climb into the other wagon from both ends when Fargo crossed the space in his long, loping stride, the Colt in his hand.

"Hold it right there," he called out softly. The drifter with one leg up at the rear of the wagon froze, the one beside him half-turning. Fargo's eyes went to the other one at the front of the wagon, saw the man's hand go for his gun as he peered around the corner of the wagon frame. The big Colt .45 exploded, a single shot, and the man's head seemed to almost fly from his body in a shatter of bone and blood as he pitched backward. Fargo dropped to one knee, an instant movement, saw the other two spin around, try to draw. His shot caught the one as he dropped back from the wagon, sent the man sprawling sideways with one foot still raised in the air. The other drifter got a shot off that passed over the Trailsman's head. It was his last shot as two slugs from the heavy Colt tore his belly apart. He clapped his hands to his groin as he staggered forward, sank down to his knees in an obscene parody of prayer, and then pitched onto his face.

Fargo had dived to one side, came up again, once more moving in automatic, trained reactions. But no shot came from the other wagon. He heard only young, high-pitched voices from inside the second Conestoga, the sounds of frantic movement. Fargo stayed low, ducked under the edge of the tarpaulin where it touched the ground. "You've got three seconds," he called, and saw Karen

9

Fisher appear at the tailgate of the wagon, step down in a high-necked cotton nightdress. The drifter came into view, right behind her, the gun pressed into the small of her back.

"I'll blast her," Fargo heard the man call, his voice nervous. He stayed behind the young woman, backing toward his horse, holding her in front of him as a shield. "Don't try anything or she gets it," the drifter said, and once again the fear and nervousness was stark in his voice.

"Let her go and you can ride out," Fargo said.

"Bullshit," the drifter snapped back.

"Boys, stay inside the wagon," Fargo heard Karen Fisher call out. She didn't come apart, he noted with a moment of passing approval. The drifter went around to the other side of his horse and Fargo watched the young woman climb into the saddle with the gun held into her side, saw the man swing up behind her, wheel the horse around, and start to back the animal away. Too close, Fargo muttered under his breath, especially in the half-light of the dawn. He watched the man back the horse another half-dozen yards, then turn, send the horse into a flying gallop.

Fargo raced for the pinto, still waiting in the line of pin cherries, vaulted into the saddle, and started after the fleeing drifter. He held the pinto back, stayed in sight, but let the drifter think he was able to gain hardly at all. He caught the man's backward glances as they raced across the gently rolling, thick grass. He let the pinto creep up a yard, held him back again. The drifter threw another glance behind, made the decision Fargo wanted him to make. He put his arm against Karen Fisher's shoulder, toppled her from the galloping horse, increased speed at once. Fargo saw the girl hit the ground on her side, roll on the soft grass, lift herself on one elbow, and shake her head. He saw her eyes find him, surprise come into them

10

as he didn't stop but raced on past her. The bottom of the nightdress had ripped, he noted, glimpsed a length of well-turned leg.

He saw the drifter look back, his surprise matching the girl's. He, too, had expected Fargo to stop, and he dug spurs into the horse's flank. He had another surprise as suddenly the pinto began to close the distance with long, easy strides as Fargo let the horse have his head. Fargo drew the Colt, waited, let the pinto close another dozen yards. He saw the man throw another glance back, fear on his face now. The drifter reached back to draw his gun and Fargo fired. The man's battered, flat-brimmed hat flew from his head and he pulled his hand from his holster, tried to flatten himself against the horse's withers. Fargo let the pinto close the remaining distance full out, fired again, and the shot almost creased the man's scalp.

"Rein up," he yelled. He saw the man yank back on the reins, the horse start to come to a halt, finally stop, snorting in deep drafts of air. The drifter straightened up in the saddle, held his hands aloft, fear in his long, drawn face. Fargo halted the pinto alongside the other horse, reached over, and took the man's gun from his holster, tossed it away. "You're smarter than your three friends," Fargo commented. "You're still alive."

The man let grim awareness reach through the fear in his face, lowered his hands. "You cut them down like nothin'," the man said. "I ain't in your class."

"You're in nobody's class, drifter," Fargo said. "You're cowshit and you're lucky you're alive. Now tell me about the girl. Why were you following her?"

"She's got a damn pot full of money on her," the man said. "I saw it when she bought those tarps. I was in Davis' store when she came in."

"So you decided to go get it," Fargo said.

"Why not?" the man muttered.

"Nothing else?" Fargo pressed.

The man frowned. "What else is there?" he asked. "She seemed like an easy mark, alone with that mess of dressed-up, pink-cheeked kids."

The man was telling the truth, Fargo knew. He wasn't the kind to come up with quick stories. "I ought to let daylight through you," Fargo said. "I'd probably be doing somebody a big favor. You're only going to make trouble somewhere, someplace." He saw the fear come into the man's eyes at once.

"No, I'm going straight, mister," the man protested. "Really, I am. This taught me a lesson, honest it did."

"Bullshit," Fargo said. "But I've got a thing about shooting stray dogs in cold blood. Start riding and don't even look back."

The man swallowed, grabbed the reins of his horse. "Sure, sure thing," he murmured, spurred the horse forward into a gallop, and raced across the sloping, rolling terrain. He didn't look back and Fargo grunted, turned the pinto around, and trotted off. Karen Fisher was a strange figure striding along the grass in her torn nightdress and she turned as she heard him riding up, come to a halt. The side of her cheek was bruised, smudged with dirt, he saw as he swung down from the pinto.

"Thank you," Karen Fisher said, her dark-blue eyes wide. "I'm most grateful to you. We all are."

"Now, you're going to tell me what the hell you're all about," Fargo said, cutting her off.

"Can we go back to the wagons first?" she asked. "I'd rather put on something proper before we talk."

"I like it this way," he said, letting his eyes take in the smooth-skinned, long line of her leg under the torn nightdress, the round high breasts that pushed the top of the nightdress out. "Start talking."

"Are you always this contrary?" Karen Fisher asked, her eyes darkening.

12

"I just saved your little ass. I can be anything I damn well please," he growled at her.

Her face set in the haughty coolness it had worn in the hotel room. "A good deed, even an exceptional one, shouldn't be used as an excuse," she said primly.

"A big mouth, even an exceptional one, can get you a long, lonely walk back," Fargo said.

She searched the lake-blue eyes and he saw her draw in a deep breath. "All right," she said. "You're a most difficult man."

"Sometimes," Fargo said. "Talk."

# 2

"You've spoken to your friend, Mr. Davis, I take it," Karen Fisher said, and Fargo nodded. "Then he told you I'm taking a wagonload of young boys up to Beulah in the Dakota Territory."

"He told me and I told him you were crazy," Fargo said.

She allowed a glance of impatience. "I'm aware there's a certain element of danger," she said.

"There's a certain element of getting dead quick," Fargo said.

A touch of grimness took hold in her face. "You're speaking of the hostiles, I presume," she said.

"I'm talking about Indians, bandits, bushwhackers, old mother nature, whatever you can dream up," Fargo said.

"Nonetheless, it is something I must do," she said.

"Why?" Fargo asked bluntly.

"These boys are in my charge. The military school they were attending burned down and left them stranded. I was the only teacher not injured. Luckily, the headmaster had just started a new school in Beulah and I'm taking the boys there," she said.

Fargo frowned at her. "Beulah's a hell of a place to start a new military academy, smack in the middle of Indian country," he said.

"I was told that Beulah is a stable, growing community

14

made up of good settlers, family people," Karen Fisher said.

"Sure as hell not what I know about it," Fargo muttered.

"Have you ever been there?" she asked.

"No, but I know some who have and they painted a different picture," he told her.

"It has obviously changed, then. Places do change, you know, grow more stable," she said somewhat severely.

"Maybe." He shrugged. "Still a crazy idea."

"Crazy or not, I must go on," she said. "Now, may we go back? The boys must be sick with worry and fear."

"I guess so," Fargo said, and felt vaguely dissatisfied with Karen Fisher's story. Nothing he could pin down except that it was sure a strange tale, yet this land was full of strange things. He swung onto the pinto, reached down, and pulled her into the saddle behind him. She had to hold on to him as he rode off and he allowed himself a small smile as he felt her breasts push into his back, warm through the thinness of the nightdress. As he reached the wagons, he saw everyone in uniform, caps smartly on each head, all lined up and faces turned toward the approaching horse. The tarpaulins were still up as a backdrop as he came to a halt and Karen Fisher slid from the saddle, the torn nightdress again showing a nicely turned, long leg. He dismounted as she faced the row of uniformed boys.

"This is Mr. Fargo, boys," she said. "We all owe him a great debt of gratitude."

Fargo glanced across at the unshaven faces, so young-looking under the large caps, each face very serious.

"Now take down the tarpaulins and get the wagons ready to travel while I dress and then talk to Mr. Fargo," Karen ordered, and they broke ranks to turn away as Karen started into the first Conestoga. "Please

15

wait at the front of the wagon for me," she called back to Fargo.

Fargo started to snap an answer, held himself back as she disappeared into the wagon. She had a way of saying things, as though she just naturally expected people to do her bidding, that rubbed him the wrong way. Maybe it just came from being a schoolteacher, he muttered to himself, but he was on the pinto when she emerged from the Conestoga. She wore the gray dress with the pink collar again and he saw the surprise in her eyes. "Are you just going to ride off?" she asked, a note of accusation in her voice.

"That's my plan," he said.

"I wanted to talk to you about staying on and helping us get to Beulah," she said, moving closer to the pinto.

He stared down at her. "Me? That drunk in the hotel room?" Fargo asked.

Her lips tightened. "I may have been hasty," she said, but there was no give in her eyes, he noted.

"Hasty?" Fargo echoed, waited.

"All right, I may have been in error," she said waspishly.

"Does that mean I shoot pretty good for a drunk?" Fargo asked blandly.

Her lips tightened further. "I said I may have been in error," she repeated.

"May have been isn't good enough, honey," Fargo said.

Her eyes flashed. "All right, I *was* in error. Will that do?" she returned.

"For now," Fargo said.

"And the name is Karen, not *honey*," she snapped. "How did you happen to be here at the proper moment?" she added, her eyes sharp on him.

"Happened to be riding this way. Saw your wagons and saw those bushwhackers. Decided to wait around and watch," Fargo said.

16

"I'm certainly grateful that you did," Karen Fisher said. "Obviously, I'm going to need help. That's why I came to you in the first place. You're obviously very good at what you do, the kind of man I need." She halted, frowned up at him. "Can't you at least get down from that saddle while we talk?" she asked testily.

"Can't see much left to talk about," Fargo said.

"I want to hire you. I was told this is the kind of thing you do. They call you the Trailsman," she said.

"They do and I don't want them to start calling me the nursemaid," Fargo said.

"I'll be the nursemaid. You will be strictly our guide. I'll pay you a hundred dollars a boy to get us there. There are twelve boys," she said.

Fargo felt his brow lifting. "Twelve hundred dollars?" He frowned. "That's mighty fancy money. These kids made of gold?"

"They come from wealthy homes. It will be written into their expenses. Will you stay on?" she asked.

"One hundred for each," Fargo mused aloud. "And if only two make it?"

"You get two hundred dollars," she said at once. "But you can't be serious about only two making it."

"Too damn serious," Fargo said, let his thoughts pull together. He'd risked life and limb for less, a lot less. He glanced hard at Karen Fisher. "If I say, No, thanks?"

"I'll go on anyway. I've no choice," she said firmly.

Fargo glanced over at the figures lined up by the other Conestoga. "Shit," he growled. "They're awful young to lose their scalps."

Karen Fisher gave him a careful glance. "Does that mean you'll go with us?" she asked.

"That'll depend on Sioux Falls," Fargo said, saw her frown. "I have to see a man who might be there," he finished.

"A man worth more than twelve hundred dollars?" she questioned.

Fargo's lake-blue eyes hardened instantly. "A lot more to me," he said, and Karen Fisher decided not to ask further.

"If you decide to go with us, there's one rule I must insist upon," she said. "These young boys are all at a very impressionable age. I must ask that you keep away from them. With all due respect, you are not the ideal role model for young boys who are being raised to be proper, clean-living, modest, and gentlemanly. In fact, I've seen no one out here who would serve as a good example for them, so I must insist they have their privacy and be left strictly to me."

"Is that the reason for those fool tarpaulins?" Fargo asked.

"Exactly. They keep out prying eyes and allow the boys their privacy, from me, as well," she said, saw the expression come into his eyes. "You disapprove, I take it?"

"Hell, it'll make folks more curious," Fargo said.

"Curious or not, it is the one condition I must insist upon," Karen answered firmly.

Fargo leaned forward in the saddle to give her a hard stare. "Now I'll give you a condition. If, and I'm saying if, I take you on, everything else is my way. No arguments, no second guesses. I call all the shots all the way."

She considered for a moment. "All right," she said, her chin lifted. "But you're still saying if. How will I know whether it's yes or no?"

Fargo stared into space for a moment, remembering the roads to Sioux Falls. "You'll pass Sioux Falls on your way, the road curves around it. Go on a mile or so past town. Make camp near the road. If it's yes, I'll come find you when I'm finished."

She considered for a moment. "I don't have much choice, do I?" she said.

He shrugged. "You can go on and not bother waiting to find out," he answered.

"We'll make camp," she said. "But I should like to see this man who's so important to you," she added tartly.

"If he's there, you can see his funeral," Fargo said, his voice soft steel. He swung the pinto around, paused to look back at her. "Some free advice. Take the three horses. The former owners won't be riding them anymore. Have three of your little gentlemen ride and lighten your wagons."

He spun the pinto around, not waiting for an answer, rode off, slowed only after he was out of sight. The road went north, just inside the edge of the Dakota Territory, all the way to Sioux Falls, and he rode easily, unhurriedly. Karen Fisher had already left his thoughts as he wondered what lay in Sioux Falls.

He couldn't grow excited any longer, not after the hundreds of false leads and disappointments, the countless towns where the search had come up fruitless. Still, he'd never stopped looking, asking, running down each rumor, trailing each possible lead. He had heard about this one while celebrating in Moosehead and, despite all the bourbon, had filed it away in his mind. It had been only a few words, a description of a man, the name of a town. But the description fit and that was enough. He had to follow through, just as he'd followed through on all the others. As he rode, the big black-haired man's lake-blue eyes turned to blue ice as his thoughts went back to that day forever seared inside him.

He had come home to the little house so lovingly built by his father, to find the scene of carnage, vicious, brutal murder, everyone dead, his pa, his ma, and his brother. But one of the killers had dropped an initialed tobacco pouch. It was proof of what he had already concluded.

The murderers were the same trio that had tried to frame his father, a Wells Fargo road agent, in a robbery scheme. Failing, they had returned to silence the one man who could identify them. Skye Fargo had been born that day, midwifed by cold-blooded murder, baptised in the blood of vengeance. He had buried his family, taken a name to forever remind him of his mission, and turned to the trail, the vow burning forever inside him.

So much had happened since, so many trails ridden, so many byways and bypaths ventured onto, and the name of Skye Fargo, the Trailsman, became known to many as the man who could track like a mountain lion, scout like an Indian, and read nature's signs like a red-tailed hawk. So much since that terrible day, he reflected now as he rode the pinto north, so many detours, so many women, and that one goal always there inside him.

He pursued one more slender thread of a lead now, yet he could do nothing else and he continued on until the day began to close down. He found a little rocky spot tucked away by itself and made camp as night came; he chewed on some cold beef jerky and washed it down with water from his canteen. He'd make Sioux Falls tomorrow and begin the business of nosing around carefully. As he stretched out on his bedroll, the sky sparkling with stars from end to end, he gave a moment to thoughts of Karen Fisher and her strange cargo. She was offering the kind of money hard to turn down, but money was damn little good if your carcass held nothing but arrows.

Her venture was sure a wild one, but this was a land of wild ventures. The land seemed a kind of contagion, turning people to dreams and hopes, dreams too strong for common sense, hopes that stampeded facts into the dirt. He'd seen it often enough, maybe not as strange a venture as hers but just as damn divorced from reality. Karen Fisher and her boys could well be just one more party to simply vanish away in the savage, relentless land. He turned on his side. There'd be time enough to decide about Karen Fisher after he saw to Sioux Falls. He fell asleep quickly, too many disappointments inside him to allow hope to keep him awake.

When morning crept over the rocks, he rose, washed in a trickle of a stream he found, and climbed onto the pinto again. It was a little past midday when he rode into Sioux Falls. The town had grown some since he'd last been there, he noted, a new, expanded general store and the main street more crowded with wagons. He made his way to the stable, first, run by a smithy. The man interrupted his work long enough to give Fargo a curt answer.

"Don't talk about my customers, stranger. That's why they come to me. I respect a man's privacy," he said.

"Fair enough," Fargo agreed, and wheeled the pinto away. It wasn't time to press anyone yet. He tried the general store, the proprietor a man with a mane of white hair that matched his white apron. The man pursed his lips and thought for a moment at Fargo's question.

"I don't know names, except for my regular customers, but there is a feller fits that description," the storekeeper said. Fargo's face remained impassive.

"Very tall, maybe six-four and thin, a long, hard face that matches the rest of him?" Fargo prodded.

"Yep, sounds like him, all right," the man said. "Comes in here once a week with a young woman, picks up groceries, mostly canned stuff."

Fargo refused to let excitement catch at him, remembering the long trail of disappointments that lay behind. "Know where I might find him?" he asked casually.

"Don't know where he might be staying in town. But I hear he's a real card shark and plays every night at the Nugget," the man said.

"Thanks, much obliged," Fargo said, and returned to the pinto outside, walked down the main street, his frown digging into his brow. The man could have a woman with

21

him. That didn't prove anything one way or the other. The Nugget lay at the near end of town, an ordinary gambling house and brothel. He peered in the window, saw two old men sweeping and setting up tables, a girl having coffee alone in one corner.

"Want something, mister?" the voice said at his elbow, and he turned to see the woman, too heavily made up, a flat face topped with tightly curled bottle-blond hair, eyes that had seen the world too much. "I'm Maddy. I run the Nugget," she said, though the explanation was unnecessary, the badge in her face.

Fargo allowed a pleasant smile. "Just looking to see when you open," he said.

"Eight o'clock, unless you can't wait that long," she said.

"I can wait." He smiled.

Her eyes went up and down the big, broad-shouldered figure. "You're a good-looking one. I'll save one of my best girls for you," she offered.

Fargo let the smile widen. "Thanks. I'll see you tonight," he said, and returned to lead the pinto off. No questions for her. Madams formed their own allegiances and questions could be quickly passed on and he didn't want that. He wanted to be sure first. He walked down the street, the Ovaro following behind him drawing admiring glances.

"*Fargo!* I'll be damned," he heard the voice call out, and he whirled, the Colt half-out of the holster instantly. "Easy, friend," the voice said, and Fargo stared at the man, the balding head with the monk's cap fringe of hair, the face still smooth despite its years.

"Jack Allison," he said.

"Jesus, you're jumpy," the man commented.

Fargo's smile relaxed. "Maybe a mite," he admitted as he took the outstretched hands.

"God, it's been years, Fargo," Jack Allison said. "Been

hearing about you, though. Still the best trailsman in the country, they say."

"You running your wagons up this far?" Fargo asked.

"Special trip here," the man answered. "No farther, though. Dakota Territory's still too wild for me. What brings you here?"

Fargo hesitated a moment, then went on. Jack Allison had been a friend of his father and he'd been there soon after it had happened. "Got a lead," the Trailsman said, knowing he needn't say more. The man's eyes widened at once. "Tall, very thin, long, thin face. Used to go by the name of Sledge," Fargo added.

Jack Allison's eyes widened further. "He still does," the man said.

"Then he's here," Fargo said, and felt the stab of excitement that caught at him, refusing denial any longer.

"Plays cards every night at the Nugget," Jack Allison said, nodding.

Fargo's eyes grew dark-blue fires in their depths. Inside, the excitement grew, surging through him. No false leads this time. The real thing, finally, one of the trio within his reach at last. He savored the thought a moment more and felt his hand clenching, moving up toward the big Colt at his side as if with a will of its own. He opened his hand, forced it to return to his side, stepped into a doorway, and pulled Allison in with him. "I hear he has a woman with him," he said.

"Never saw her," the man said. "I've been having a drink at the Nugget every night this week and he's always alone. He card-sharks all night and I guess sleeps off the day. Maybe the woman stays in the hotel with him. Hell, he's a cheatin' player, but nobody's been able to catch him at it."

Fargo lost himself in thought for a moment, decided not to try to track the man down at the hotel. He'd wait for the chance to see the man for himself first. He caught

23

Jack Allison peering at him. "Where?" the man asked, reading his thoughts.

"At the Nugget, tonight," Fargo said.

"Anything I can do?" the man asked.

"Not now," Fargo said, his face made of stone. Allison nodded as the big black-haired man strode to the pinto and swung into the saddle. Only a few hours to go, Fargo noted as the sun began to lower across the horizon. He'd do his waiting alone; he rode from town, found an old shack, and sank down behind it, leaning against the weathered, half-rotted boards. Slowly, the dusk came, turned into night, and the silent figure behind the shack sat motionless until, abruptly, it rose, swung onto the big pinto in one graceful motion, and headed the horse back toward Sioux Falls.

The time had come, the hours passing as though they were minutes. Fargo rode slowly, reached the main street, moved toward the hum of noise from the gambling broth-el. There was no need to hurry now. If it really was the same Sledge, this would be the night of reckoning, the first of those yet to come. He dismounted, draped the pinto's reins across the hitching post in front of the Nugget, and made his way along the side of the frame structure until he found the side door. Silently, he let himself inside, found a dim hallway. He saw a doorway, set off from the main room by a beaded curtain, and he moved to it, pressed his eye between two rows of beads, and scanned the big room. The Nugget was already crowded with the girls, drinkers, seekers, and gamblers clustered around their tables. Slowly, his ice-blue eyes moved along the tables lining the walls where a half-dozen games of poker and red dog were in progress. He felt the sharp intake of breath as his glance came to a halt at the last table near the window. His eyes riveted on the man dealing, the thin, long face with the harsh eyes one of the three faces indelibly etched into his mind.

"Sledge," he murmured softly. No more wondering. No more false leads. Sledge, here, in his sight. Fargo felt the ice forming inside him, the cold hatred that he had carried for so long crystallizing inside him until he was filled with a cold fire.

Jack Allison was in the room somewhere. He'd want to be there at the showdown, when yesterday came to today. Fargo parted the curtain, moved out into the room, and he caught the madam's glance, frowning as she saw him step from behind the beaded drape. He moved along the edge of the tables until he was almost at the one by the big plate-glass window. The harsh-eyed man with the long, thin face was gathering in an armful of chips.

"Looks like another lucky night for me," he heard the man say.

"Guess again, Sledge," Fargo said quietly, saw the man look up at him at once, no recognition in his eyes. The years had changed him some, he knew, and he had always been in the background, youngest of the family. He wasn't surprised that Sledge didn't recognize him. Yet the man saw something, felt an intuitive awareness of danger, and it showed in the harsh eyes, a moment of uncertainty.

"Do I know you, stranger?" Sledge said.

"Better than you think," Fargo said, and the man's brow furrowed. "Remember the Wells Fargo job, Sledge?" Fargo asked softly, and watched the flash of surprise course through the man's face, fear instant on its heels. Sledge forced the fear from his face, pushed back in his chair, met the big black-haired man's icy eyes.

"You're not making any sense to me, stranger," he said.

"You're a goddamn liar, Sledge," Fargo said, his voice hardly more than a whisper. Out of the corner of his eye he saw the others nearby moving to the sides hurriedly. Sledge half-smiled, shook his head, started to lean forward in the chair, and moving with surprising quickness,

25

dropped to his knees behind the table. Fargo snapped the Colt out of the holster, fired, the shot splintering the edge of the table. The man fired back from below the table but not moving into danger, his shot aimed upward, shattering the kerosene-lamp chandelier directly overhead. Fargo half-twisted, dived to one side as burning bits of kerosene and shattered glass crashed down. He whirled back, on one knee, in time to see Sledge's long form diving through the plate-glass window, headfirst, carrying a shower of smashed glass with him.

Fargo leaped to his feet, raced to the shattered window, and pulled back as the bullet whistled through the broken space of the window. Dropping down, he ducked forward again, saw the streaking figure disappear around the corner of a building. Fargo leaped through the broken window, landed on his feet outside, ran to the corner, and whirled around it, the Colt upraised, ready to fire. But the passageway by the building was empty and the shouts from the Nugget drowned out any sound of fleeing footsteps. His mouth a grim line, the Trailsman spun, ran down the edge of the main street, staying by the building line. He passed the weathered sign outside the hotel, kept going. Sledge wouldn't stop to collect the woman, he knew. He had just reached the edge of the stable when he heard the sound of the horse from inside, a wild snort and then hooves digging into a galloping start. Fargo gathered his powerful leg muscles, ran another half-dozen steps, slowed, pressed his boots hard into the soft soil, and leaped, up and forward. He was in midair as the horse bolted out of the stable, Sledge bent low in the saddle, blood streaming from his forehead from glass cuts.

Fargo slammed into the man in midair, grabbed hold of an arm, felt himself yanked forward by the momentum of the horse, and then he was falling, still hanging on to his quarry, and he felt the man going with him, sliding from the saddle. Fargo twisted his body to land on his side as the horse raced on, released his grip to avoid breaking an arm, hit the ground, and felt the other man land with a thud almost beside him. He rolled, got to one knee, shook his head, and saw Sledge starting to rise. Fargo dived at the man as the killer tried to draw his gun, crashed a blow to the man's face, but his timing was off and he felt his knuckles only glance the jaw. Sledge fired off a shot from half on his back, a wild bullet, and Fargo rolled, came up with the big Colt in his hand. He fired, letting go with every shot still in the chamber, and with each thunderous blast went all the pent-up hate and vengeance he had carried for so long. Each blazing shot a payment, a debt made good, a promise fulfilled, justice done. He watched the heavy slugs smash into the man, chest, neck, face, until the figure seemed a grisly fountainpiece spouting red in all directions.

Fargo rose from his knee, holstered the Colt, and stared at the long figure, twisted and riddled in death as the crowd came quickly, pouring out of the gambling house to stand in awed silence. The sheriff arrived soon after, relief in his face at a situation already finished. He was, Fargo saw at once, a man who timed his arrivals after trouble was over. There were few questions. Everyone had seen Sledge drop behind the table and draw his gun first, and as Fargo turned, he saw Jack Allison nearby. The man's eyes were wide and he nodded slowly, fell into step beside Fargo as the big black-haired man returned to the Nugget, sat down at a table, and ordered a bottle of bourbon. Jack Allison eased into the chair next to him as one of the girls brought the bottle and the house began to fill up again.

Fargo poured a glass for Jack, raised his own in a salute. "To yesterday," he said, and downed the bourbon. He waited till Jack Allison finished his bourbon. "Now you can do something for me," he said. "Get the woman and bring her here while I enjoy my bourbon."

27

"Sure, Fargo," Jack said. "I figure she's at the hotel."

Fargo poured another shot glass for himself as Allison disappeared through the double doors of the house. The Nugget was quickly settling back to its normal pace. None knew, and few would care, that they had seen the end of a cold-blooded, murdering killer. Death in this country was a passing nod. The moment of violence had come and gone, and existence went on. A callous and barbaric attitude, some would say, but Fargo knew it for what it was, a necessity, the only way to exist in a land where savagery and death were constant companions. He sipped at his drink and saw the bottle-blond madam of the place moving toward him. She halted at the table, peered sharply at him.

"I don't know why, but I figured you for trouble when I saw you this afternoon," she told him, one hand on her hip.

"It's over," he said. "He was dead a long time ago. He just didn't know it till now."

"I'll see that Sheriff Sam gives me the money out of his pockets for the price of my window," the woman said truculently.

"You do that," Fargo answered, and was glad to see her walk away. He poured another bourbon for himself, had taken the first sip of it when he saw Jack Allison appear with the woman in tow. Younger than he'd expected, she was a washed-out blond with her natural looks pretty well erased by wear and tear. She followed Allison to the table, apprehension in her face.

"Sit down," Fargo said pleasantly enough, watched her slide into a chair, her eyes on him. He took in the cotton dress, a small gray-flecked plaid that rested on smallish breasts and a thin, angular figure. "How long did you know him?" Fargo asked almost casually.

"A month or two," she said, saw the question form in the big man's eyes. "All right, two months," she amended.

"Drink?" Fargo offered, and she nodded gratefully. "Where'd you meet him?" Fargo asked as he poured the bourbon for her.

"In Elkhorn, down Iowa way. I wanted out of Elkhorn and he was a ticket," she said, drawing deep of the whiskey.

"Did he ever talk about two friends of his, name of Maklin and Cresh?" Fargo asked.

"Not to me," she said.

"Think hard about this," Fargo said, leaning forward. She saw the change come into his eyes and blinked back.

"Honest, mister, he never did," she said. "Once, he talked about sometime hooking up again with some old friends, that's all."

Fargo's eyes stayed on her. "He name a place, a time?"

"No, honest, he didn't. He just talked about it one day, just in passing," she said. "Kind of a stray thought." Fargo's eyes stayed on the girl and she moved, suddenly uncomfortable. "Honest, mister. I've got no reason to hold back, not now. He can't hurt me for talking now."

Fargo let his breath slide out and sat back in the chair. She was right, of course. She'd no reason to hold back. She knew nothing of value, he was certain. The other two would hang on to life a little longer and the search would go on. Their time would come. "Have another drink," he said to the girl. "Relax. Enjoy yourself. I'll be on my way soon." He watched the girl drink eagerly, cast a quick glance at him.

"Maybe you could take me along," she suggested with a sideway glance.

"I travel alone," Fargo said.

Frank Allison cut in. "I'm heading east with some wagons. You can ride along," he said, and the girl's smile was a sudden flash of gratitude.

"Thanks," she said. "Count on me."

Fargo watched her visibly grow less tense and listened

29

idly as she began to tell Jack Allison about herself. It was a story he'd heard often enough from others, different faces and different places, but the rest the same, webs of defeat and despair that trap. He had another bourbon and felt his own tensions drop away. No celebration mood but a quiet satisfaction, a down payment made on a promise. He found himself talking about old times with Jack Allison, old rememberings that seemed to fit the mood. The young woman knew how to be a pleasant listener and Jack bought another round of drinks. Fargo was drawing on his when he saw her, glimpsing the high pink collar first as she halted just inside the doorway, lips drawn tight, her eyes sweeping the Nugget.

He saw her brow lower as she spotted him, watched Karen Fisher start to make her way toward him, brushing past an outstretched arm, sweeping around a knot of boisterous drunks, coming to a halt at the table, fire in her eyes. "You really have no sense of responsibility at all, do you?" she hissed. "You were going to give me a decision. I've been waiting for hours and hours."

Fargo flicked a glance at Jack Allison and the girl, saw them looking on in surprise. As Karen's voice rose, he saw others turning to watch, some with growing grins. "I got tired waiting," Karen Fisher snapped out. "I decided to see for myself. I expected I'd find you in this place." She flung a glance at the girl. "So this is your important meeting," she said, sniffing disdainfully. "I'm waiting with a wagon full of young boys for you to give me a decision and you're whoring it up here."

She was making no effort to keep her voice down and still others had turned to watch and listen. Fargo drained the last of his bourbon, met the fury of her eyes.

"Well, are you sober enough to give me an answer?" she snapped. He saw that she was too caught up in her own self-righteous fury to read the change in his eyes. "I'm waiting," she demanded, still not catching the cold

30

quiet settling into his face. He rose, slowly, almost with resignation, then moving with the swiftness of a hawk diving onto a hare, he scooped her into his arms and flung her over his shoulder. He heard her scream of surprise as he started to walk with her, the roar of laughter following him drowning out her screams of protest.

He strode from the Nugget with her, Jack Allison leading the pack following. Outside, he marched with his kicking, furiously screaming bundle to the water trough a half-dozen yards from the gambling house. With a shrug of his shoulder, he dropped her into the trough. The splash as she hit sent a small cascade of water spilling over the sides of the trough, and the explosion of laughter from the onlookers all but drowned out her gargled scream of rage.

He was on the pinto, starting to wheel the horse away, as she pulled herself to her feet inside the trough, dripping wet. "Damn you, Fargo," she screamed. "You come back here." Fargo turned the pinto and rode off, not looking back, her screams sputtering off to gasped, breathless rage. He rode on unhurriedly, moving along the road, passing the two Conestogas about a mile out of town, the tarpaulins strung up from them to nearby trees. He went on, perhaps another mile until he found a little nook between a pair of chinquapins that fitted their name, Indian for "large." He dismounted, set out his bedroll, and curled up on it. He stayed awake awhile to let the events of the night settle. One down, two more to go, he thought. In time, all in time. Whatever the detours and byroads, wherever the trails took him, they'd one day lead to that final reckoning. Till then, he'd wait, watch, live. He turned on his side, slept as the night winds blew away the memories.

# 3

The sound of the wagons woke him and he pulled himself up on one elbow, blinked in the morning sun, focused on the two Conestogas moving along the road, a capped and uniformed figure driving each. Karen Fisher, riding a thick-bodied bay a dozen yards ahead of the wagons, spotted the pinto by the chinquapins and Fargo saw her turn the bay, head toward him. He lay down again, put his hands behind his head, stayed that way as he listened to the sound of the bay come up to a halt.

"Watch your mouth, honey," he said, looking up at the blue sky. "I can always find another water trough."

"My offer still stands," he heard her say, her voice crisp. "Yes or no, that's all I want to hear."

Fargo half-turned, brought his arms down from behind his head, and raised himself to one elbow to look at her. She wore a dark-green checked shirt and black riding britches, looked trim and compact.

"You're surprised?" she asked with a touch of acid.

"Yes," he admitted.

"Don't let it go to your head," she said. "I wouldn't ask you to take me around the corner." He waited, asked with his eyes. "I can't just think of myself," she went on. "I have to think of the boys. I owe them the best chance I can give them and, unfortunately, that means your help." She paused for a moment. "Twelve hundred dollars is still a great deal of money," she said.

"So it is," Fargo agreed.

"Do you want it or do I go on alone?" she remarked.

Fargo let a deep sigh escape him, pulled himself to his feet. She had her own brand of gutsiness, crazy or not, he decided. "Go on with your wagons. I'll catch up to you," he growled.

She held her eyes on him, making certain she understood, then wheeled the horse around and cantered back to the waiting wagons. Fargo used his canteen to wash as the wagons moved on out of sight, found a stand of rum cherries, and breakfasted on them. Finally, he swung onto the pinto and rode up the road. When he came into sight of the two Conestogas, the road was barely a road, drifting off into a rutted pathway, and he saw the uniformed figures inside both the wagons. A hand waved at him as he rode past, drew up alongside Karen as she rode ahead of the wagons. He raised one hand and halted, heard the wagons roll to a stop behind. His eyes swept the land to the west and to the north, semiarid in spots, long plains bordered by rolling hills and, in the unseen distance, the towering rise of the Black Hills.

"We turn here and head west," he said, and shot a quick glance at Karen Fisher. "Last chance to change your mind," he added.

She met his glance evenly. "Everyone has had a good breakfast. They know we won't be stopping till evening, except to rest the horses," she said in answer.

He nodded, raised his arm, and motioned forward as he moved the pinto into a gentle canter. He slowed to a walk soon and Karen Fisher came up beside him. He watched the way her breasts, high and full, bounced primly in unison as she rode.

"I hope you've told those kids of yours what they might be up against on this trip," Fargo remarked.

"I've told them it could be a harsh, difficult, and dangerous trip," she said.

33

Fargo made a snorting sound. "Schoolteacher words," he spit out.

"Just what does that mean?" she snapped back.

"No guts in them. Textbook talk, all neat and orderly. They say, but they don't tell," Fargo returned.

"I suppose you think I ought to have told them details of how they might be scalped, murdered, or heaven-knows-what-else. I hardly think scaring them into sleeplessness will accomplish anything positive."

"It might have given them a chance to say, No, thanks," Fargo said, and saw the quick flare in her glance.

"The decision was mine to make," she snapped. "And I expect that you will keep me fully informed of anything that you think may happen."

"You ever try not talking like a schoolteacher?" he asked evenly.

Her brown hair tossed as she looked quickly at him and he saw her bite down on her lips. "I'm sorry. Force of habit," she said. "I don't mean to sound bossy, but I do want to be kept informed."

"Maybe," he allowed, and she frowned.

"Why maybe?" she asked.

"Sometimes it's best not to know too much out here," Fargo told her mildly, saw her wrestling with the answer. "Ruins the digestion," he added, and the moment of soberness touching her eyes told him she understood.

"I still want to know," she said stubbornly. "I've heard that some Indian tribes are really quite friendly."

"Some are, only not the ones you'll likely be meeting in the Dakota Territory," Fargo said.

"I thought we'd be meeting only the Sioux," she said.

"You've been hearing bits and pieces. This part of the territory is mostly Sioux but not all. The Sioux range all the way to the Rockies. But then you'll find the Assiniboins coming over from Montana Territory and the Wind River Shoshoni moving eastward. Sometimes you can run into Arikara and Mandan. Once in a while, some Crow, but they usually stay west."

"And it doesn't matter which ones we meet?" she asked.

"Not unless you care a lot about what kind of carving is on the arrow in your gut," he said.

She fell silent, stayed that way as they rode, and he didn't tell her that there was much more than the Indian to threaten them in the savage land. His lake-blue eyes scanned the horizon, looking for a spiral of dust, a sudden flight of prairie chickens, a circle of slow-wheeling vultures. He decided to travel along the edge of the hills as long as possible before moving onto the open plains. He stopped twice to rest the horses, rode a hundred yards ahead to peer along the ridgeline of the hills. He glanced back to see the capped, uniformed figures, Karen with them, changing two of the horses in the lead wagon for the mounts taken from the bushwhackers. The boys moved with quick, military precision, and were back inside the wagons in minutes.

Fargo waved them forward and they continued on until the gray-blue of dusk began to tint the sky. He led the wagons to a good stand of box elders and halted a distance up the side of a hill as Karen rode up to him. "You'll bed down there with the wagons. I'm going up atop the ridge," he told her.

She followed his gaze up to the crest of the ridgeline. "I do want privacy for the boys, but you needn't carry it that far," she said, eyeing the distance up to the ridgeline.

"It doesn't have a damn thing to do with their privacy," Fargo said. "You've a real knack for coming up with wrong answers." Her lips tightened as he laughed. "Now you better get set up before the light goes," he told her, and she turned her horse and cantered back to the wagons.

Fargo moved the pinto up the hill to the top of the

ridge as the gray-blue deepened into dark purple, then to the black of night. He found a comfortable spot on the top of the ridge, behind a wide, thick log that lightning had once felled and still bore the blackened shear marks. When dawn came, he would have a clear view of the land below, as far on as the eye could see. The Sioux liked to ride in the early day, before the sun grew too hot and scorched the prairie. Fargo settled himself behind the heavy log and made a small fire of slow-burning green branches. He could see down to the bottom of the hill where a faint glow showed the tarpaulins had been strung up in a circle again; he sat back, took off shirt, then trousers and boots, spread the clothes over the log to air out. The night had turned warm, and with the small fire he was entirely comfortable in his shorts.

He lay back, watched the stars appear, always sudden, as if some unseen, giant hand had flung them across the sky. He was relaxed when he heard the sound, the rustle of brush from halfway down the ridge. His hand went to the holster against the log, drew the Colt as he waited, listening, eyes narrowed. He heard the sound again, let his muscles relax, and put the gun back into the holster. No wild creature, no cougar prowling, not all that heavy-footed clumping, and he was waiting, his eyes on her as she emerged from the shadows into the dim light of the fire. She carried a tin bowl, covered with a battered lid.

"I brought you some thick soup," she said, kneeling down, setting the bowl on the ground. He moved forward to her, took the lid from the bowl, and drew in the rich aroma. He saw the spoon half-hidden in the bowl, pulled it out, and moved to sit down. "You could put on trousers," he heard her say sternly.

He glanced up at her, saw her look away from the hard-muscled body, the powerful curve of his thighs. "You've been teaching and living in a boys' academy and

36

you're still bothered by a little naked male skin?" he re-marked.

"The boys maintain their privacy. I've always seen to that," she said stiffly, casting another quick glance at him and looking off into the darkness again. "Besides, it's quite different with you."

"It sure is. Glad you noticed." Fargo grinned. She continued to look away and he pulled his trousers from the log, drew them on, and sat down with the bowl again. "Is that better, honey?" he commented.

"Thank you," she said, returned her eyes to him.

He ate the soup hungrily, found it held potato and pieces of stew meat, finally finished, and returned the lid to the pot.

"Mighty obliged," he said, leaning back. "Aren't you afraid you'll spoil me?" he asked with a half-smile.

"You needn't fear that," she returned coolly. "This will hardly be a nightly event. However, sharing is part of this kind of venture, I believe."

"So it is," Fargo said, held back from telling her that she might well be sharing pain, hardship, even death. "You always strung out so tight?" he asked casually.

Karen Fisher fixed a disdainful glance on him. "I am not strung out tight, to use your unfortunate way of saying things," she answered. "I am a believer in self-discipline."

"Self-discipline's one thing, shriveled up's another," he said mildly. She flashed anger in her eyes, picked up the bowl and spun on her heel, stalked off. "Have your boys ready to roll soon after dawn," he called after her as she disappeared into the dark. He put his trousers back over the log, lay down on his bedroll, and listened to the sound of her making her way back. He smiled to himself. She was a coiled-up wire. She had to work hard at holding that self-discipline together. It might still be a rewarding trip in many ways. He closed his eyes and slept as the warm wind rustled through the brush.

The first pink line stretched across the dawn sky, and on the ridge the big black-haired man crouched as he watched the new day unfold. Slowly, his eyes moved back and forth across the land below, trailing along the edge of the hills, scanning the lay of the prairie. He caught the quick, darting movements of small wild creatures, ferrets and prairie dogs, a morning fox and the ever-present jack-rabbits. He watched a half-dozen prairie antelope bound over the land as though they had legs made of steel springs, and finally he rose, went to where the pinto waited, and mounted. The land held no danger visible to the eye. It was but a momentary indication, though, he knew, a message of limited nature, meaning only that danger and death were not in the immediate vicinity. But in this land, danger was a presence, never far away, always waiting, lurking, watching for a mistake, a moment's lapse.

He started down the ridge to where the capped and uniformed figures were just loading the tarpaulins into the wagons. Karen, on the thick-bodied mare, rode forward to meet him as the boys began clambering into the wagons. "We move out onto the prairie," he told her. "It'll cut two days from our riding time and we have to do it sooner or later, anyway," he told her. He waved the wagons forward, set a pace slightly faster than the day before.

Karen rode beside him and followed his gesture as he pointed to a trail of unshod pony tracks. "Sioux," he remarked, and saw alarm flood into her face. "Old tracks. Nothing to be concerned about," he added.

"How do you know they're old tracks?" she questioned.

"The plains dust has half-filled the deeper marks," he said. He lifted his head, grimaced at the low-flying clouds

38

and the puffs of hot wind that came at him. A storm was trying to gather itself somewhere.

"We could use water for the wagon kegs," Karen said. "I don't suppose we'll come to any out here."

"We'll be getting to water right soon," he said.

She half-turned to him. "How do you know that?" She frowned.

He gestured to a flight of birds that swooped ahead of them through the air. "Those cactus wrens. They're on their way to water. We'll just follow them."

"How can you know? They could be flying away from water," she pressed.

"Birds fly to water in the early morning, away from it in late afternoon," Fargo told her.

"How do you learn all these things? Did you have a teacher?" she asked.

"Nature's the best teacher in the world. Watching, listening, remembering, that's the heart of it," he said.

"But not everyone picks it up the way you have," she said.

"No, not everyone," he agreed. "Some cougars hunt better than others. Some men screw better than others. Some folks look while others see."

"Perhaps some men are simply more animal than others," she said, turned a bland glance at him, and he allowed a smile.

"Might just be," he agreed. "If you figure that punches into me, you're all wrong. I wouldn't want to be any other way."

"I imagine not," she said stiffly as he quickened to a canter, pulled away from her. It was a little less than an hour when they came to the water, a shallow prairie creek fed by an underground spring, but the water was fresh and clean. Fargo stayed in the saddle, watched from a distance as the boys filled the big water kegs hung from the sides of the wagons. They worked quickly in their caps and uniforms, three to a keg and having trouble at that. The military academy had done little to build muscle apparently. When they finished, he set off again at a slower pace, still frowning at the gusts of hot wind that continued to blow, fitful, restless air. He didn't like it, wished it would make its mind up.

Karen rode alongside him part of the time, back with the wagons the rest of the time, and afternoon was wearing away when he felt the pinto shaking its hind left leg. He dismounted, lifted the hoof, and uttered a soft curse as Karen rode up. "He's picked up a hoof full of broken pebbles. They've stuck into the frog," Fargo told her. "I'll have to clean them out and that'll take a while. You keep going. I'll catch up to you when I'm finished."

She nodded, but he caught the moment of uncertainty in her face. "You keep riding point," he said. "If you see anything you don't like, hightail it back here and fetch me."

She wheeled the bay around as Fargo fished into his saddlebag for the hoof-pick he carried. The two Conestogas passed and a half-dozen hands waved at him. He waved back, rummaged some more until he found the implement, and began the task of cleaning out the soft part of the hoof. It was slow, painstaking work that had to be done right. One sharp piece of broken pebble left embedded would work deeper into the frog and cause real trouble. He'd just finished, a little more than a half-hour later, was sponging off the frog when he heard the sound of galloping hooves, looked up to see Karen racing toward him on the bay.

"Sioux," she screamed. "On the horizon." She reined to a halt, and he vaulted into the saddle, swung the pinto around, and galloped off as Karen followed. When he reached sight of the two Conestogas, both halted, he flew past, galloping on as Karen raced behind him. He came into sight of the cloud of dust directly ahead, long, low, spreading to almost fill the horizon. He pulled the pinto up, waited as Karen reached him, and he held his glance on her. The fear accented the delicate loveliness of her face, adding depth to the planes of her cheekbones, and he watched the way her breasts pushed hard against the shirt with every deep breath.

"Well?" She frowned.

"No Sioux," he said calmly, saw her frown deepen.

"What then?" she asked.

He waved the wagons forward and cantered on, heard her coming after him, felt her frowning glances as she caught up to him. He cantered on, not answering, as the dust cloud lifted some, grew thinner as they neared it, and the dark-brown mass came into view, taking on shape, then form to become a huge herd of closely packed bison.

"There's your Sioux," he said as he halted. "All the Sioux in the Dakota Territory put together wouldn't raise that much dust. They'd never surprise a blind man if they did."

He watched the chagrin flood into her face. "I'm sorry. I feel so terribly stupid," she said.

"Don't. You did right by coming back for me," he said.

"Kindness?" she asked, her brows lifting. "Sensitivity? You surprise me."

"Honesty. It was a mistake most people would have made," Fargo said, and returned his eyes to the herd of bison. A big bull detached himself from the rest, turned to face the two horses, his little eyes gleaming out of his massive head, the huge, thickly furred shoulders a monument of sheer power. A second bull did the same and Fargo felt the gust of hot wind blow across his face. One big bull pawed the ground with his right forefoot and Fargo ignored the display of belligerence as he watched the rest of the tremendous herd moving within itself. Like a riptide of massive, brown forms, they moved back and forth slowly in opposite directions inside the main body of the herd.

"What is it?" he heard Karen ask, watching his narrowed eyes scanning the herd.

"They're restless. Edgy," Fargo said. "A calm, steady herd moves together, drifting along as a mass." He pulled his lips back, aware of what was making the bison edgy. The gusty winds, the restless, incipient feel of turbulence caught at them, and as with all wild creatures, they felt nature's warning signs. He listened to the sounds coming from the center of the herd, no calm lowing, not even lusty bellowing, but an uneasy, low moaning punctuated by an occasional sharp growling roar.

The wagons came up, every capped head peering out at the great herd.

Fargo's glance went to the lowering sky. "We'll keep to this side of them," he said to Karen Fisher.

"Are we going to try to go around them?" she asked.

"No, there are too many. It'd take us way into dark. We'll move on and they'll drift their way. We'll be able to move across the prairie by morning," Fargo said. "Move the wagons on, very slow and easy."

He edged the pinto a few yards closer to the bison, let the big bulls take a few steps forward to glower at him. They kept their little mean eyes on him as the wagons began to roll on; he moved the pinto a few steps back and forward. Two of the bisons raised their huge heads at the creak of the wagon wheels and Fargo pushed the pinto forward, regained their attention. The vast herd stretched out as far as he could see and the huge bisons seemed to symbolize the untamed land, malignant danger waiting to explode, beauty wrapped in power, forces that could burst forth in raw, uncontrollable savagery. He saw the herd did move, a very slow, drifting progress to the east, and he guessed it would take them three or more hours to travel a few miles down prairie.

The wagons had rolled on now; Fargo turned the pinto very slowly, and the big bulls waved their massive heads from side to side and pawed the ground. Fargo rode off slowly, staying a dozen yards from the edge of the herd until he caught up to the wagons, moved alongside Karen as she rode point. He watched the fearful glances she cast at the mass of buffalo. "Just keep moving, easy and steady," he murmured. The night was closing down fast and his eyes scanned the horizon, fastened on the distant shape of a three-pronged stone hillock rising up from the flatland. He strained his eyes at the shape, too far away to reach before dark, almost at the horizon line. The pronged hillocks, ancient rock growths, dotted the prairies like barren sanctuaries, monuments to geological history. Fargo fixed the location of the tall prongs of rock, almost invisible in the last dim light. It would make a good landmark for taking bearings in the morning.

The night closed in quickly and Fargo kept the wagons slowly rolling, finally passing the tip of the giant herd, a few stragglers standing away from the main bulk of the herd. He continued on, letting the sounds from the bisons grow dim. "It's been a long day," he heard Karen say. "The boys are very tired."

"Not yet," Fargo said brusquely. "I want more distance between that herd and us." He continued on westward, wished for more light, but the scudding, low clouds allowed only ocassional flashes of moonlight. When a break finally came in the clouds, the moon flooding down with blue-gray light, he peered back across the prairie. The herd was no longer in sight, but he continued on for another half-hour before calling a halt. Karen had gone back to ride beside the Conestogas and Fargo rode on for another hundred yards after he signaled a halt, swung down from the pinto, and watched the moon continue to play hide-and-seek behind the fast-moving clouds. He took down his bedroll as the wind continued to blow in hot, sudden gusts, still restless, still ominous.

The clouds let the moonlight through for another spell and Fargo saw the tarpaulins being strung up between the two wagons, shifted his gaze to squint across the prairie. It was a silent, empty place now, gray under the fretful moonlight. He turned as the clouds took away the light again; he found enough dry bits of prairie grass and wood to make a small fire and brew a mug of coffee to wash down the cold beef jerky. He sat in silence, finished the sparse meal, letting his eyes sweep the plains with every brief moment of moonlight. He doused his little fire with a handful of dirt when he'd done with it, peered back to the wagons, and saw the lone figure standing by the nearest Conestoga, the wind blowing a nightdress. Karen, peering out over the prairie, he reckoned, watched as the dim figure moved, climbed into the wagon. The clouds returned and the hot wind swirled over him. He frowned, took out his oilskin, and placed it within arm's reach as he lay down on the bedroll. He slept quickly, the body demanding respite from the long day in the saddle.

He had no idea how long he'd slept when the thunderclap woke him, a tremendous, sharp explosion of sound. He sat up, caught the second flash of lightning as it created a great blue-white crack in the sky, followed by another crash of thunder. He waited for the rain to come, but only the gusts of hot wind swirled over him and he stretched out again on his back, his head resting on the ground, his eyes staring up at the ink-black sky. He'd lain back but for a few moments when the frown dug into his brow and he felt the wave of vibration course through the ground under his head. He turned onto his side at once, pressed his ear down onto the ground. Another wave of vibration coursed through the ground and he waited, kept his ear against the soil, timed the third wave of vibration that came from the ground.

Uttering an oath, he leaped to his feet, swept the bed-roll and his oilskins together, and was in the saddle in seconds, digging heels into the pinto, and the horse shot forward at once. He was yelling at the top of his lungs and the double-edged throwing knife was in his hand as he raced toward the wagons.

"Roll out. Everybody, dammit," he shouted. "Get those wagons rolling." He swept past the first tarpaulin, still shouting, slashed out with the knife to sever the rope holding it, raced on to the next and slashed that one to the ground. "Out, dammit. Roll those wagons," he yelled.

Karen's head came out of the first Conestoga. "What is it? What's the matter?" she called out. He saw other capped heads starting to peer from the wagons.

"Stampede," he yelled back. "Move the damn wagons." He wheeled the pinto, slashed the last rope holding the tarpaulins.

"Don't," he heard Karen cry. "We need those."

"Forget the damn tarps. Move or you'll need nothing but a shroud."

He reined up, turned the pinto, and looked back across the blackness of the moonless prairie. There was nothing to see yet, but straining his ears, he could pick up the distant rumbling sound. Turning the pinto again, he saw the frenzied activity inside the Conestogas, and Karen, just buttoning the green-checked shirt, was mounting the bay. Two capped and uniformed figures appeared on the driver's seat of each wagon, one taking the reins, the other the whip.

"Roll them," Fargo yelled, and saw the Conestogas start forward. He rode forward to where Karen sat her horse, peered into the blackness ahead. The three-pronged rock hillocks had risen directly ahead of the horizon and he waved the wagons forward, hoping he headed in the right direction. Another flash of lightning split the sky and, for an instant, gave him his bearings as he glimpsed the distant spires of rock. Too damn distant, he thought silently. "Move," he yelled back. "Use those whips."

The sound of the whips cracking through the air answered just as the first onslaught of rain came, flinging itself into his face as if thrown from some giant bucket. The Conestogas were rolling all out now, the two teams of horses driving hard, and Fargo raced the pinto alongside Karen. The rain came in sudden gusts, then almost halted, returned again. Fargo looked behind, across the great darkness of the prairie. The herd was still out of sight, but the low rumble had grown louder, beginning to roll across the ground, taking on new strength every second. The rain suddenly halted and the fast-flying clouds broke to let moonlight rush into the breach. Fargo leaned forward in the saddle, trying to get a bearing on the distant hillocks again. Behind him, the sound was beginning to fill the air, thousands of pounding hooves blending into one shuddering roar. He flung another glance back and suddenly the flat prairie was rolling in the distance, a black line moving up and down breaking the flatness of the land.

"Move it," Fargo yelled. "Hit those whips, dammit." He was straining forward, trying to find the hillocks when the shouts of young, high voices pierced the night, cries of fright and alarm. He wheeled the pinto in a tight circle, saw the second Conestoga almost going over, tilted hard to one side as the two wheels on that side were caught in a deep, dry-bed creek rut. "Shit," Fargo cursed. "Keep going," he yelled at Karen and the other wagon as he raced back to the second Conestoga. The two boys managed to pull it to a halt, still upright, as he reached it, leaped down from the saddle.

"Everybody out. Lend a hand," Fargo shouted as he put his shoulder under the frame of the body. He felt the other uniformed figure crowding alongside him and two capped heads appeared just in front of where he stood, put shoulder under the frame of the wagon. "Lift. Get your shoulders into it," he called out. The boys next to him pushed hard, heads pressed against the side of the heavy Conestoga. Their caps fell off as Fargo, his face strained, pushed upward with every bit of his strength. He felt the wheel begin to lift out of the creekbed just as the blond hair cascaded down from where the cap had held it in place. "Hit the whip," he shouted to the two on the driver's seat and felt the horses pull, the wheel take hold and lift itself from the rut.

Slowly, Fargo straightened up, stared at the shock of blond hair, moved his eyes past it to where a cascade of light-brown hair tumbled from the second figure. They turned to him, the blond with deep brown eyes, the brown-haired one gazing out of light-blue orbs. He half-turned, stared at the other uniformed figures, three others without their caps, hair falling to their shoulders. "Girls," he heard himself say.

"I'm Chrissie," the blond said.

"I'm Joanie," the brown-haired one added.

"Girls," Fargo repeated in a half-whisper. "You're all girls." The blond nodded. "Goddamn," Fargo rasped. "*Goddamn!*" He wanted to explode, to roar out in fury, but there wasn't time for anything but running; beyond the blond figure of Chrissie, the great prairie was now a bobbing, seething mass, blacker than the night, and the ground shook under his feet. "Into the wagon," he yelled. "Hit the whip." He whirled at the others. "Two of you take the extra horses," he ordered as he whipped out his knife, cut the tethers holding the two horses to the wagon. A black-haired girl pulled herself up on one horse, a brunette on the other. Two less for the wagon to pull, he muttered to himself and leaped onto the pinto. The wagon was racing off and the moon appeared through a break in the clouds.

The buffalo were all too clear, racing closer, too damn fast, and he saw the face of thundering death reaching out for him. He raced the pinto after the Conestoga, caught up to the wagon. The girl on the reins was struggling. "Give 'em their heads," he yelled at her. "Let 'em out." He raced on to the lead wagon, only a dozen yards ahead now, Karen racing the big-bodied bay alongside it, and drew up to her. He flung another glance behind. No bobbing, seething mass now, but buffalo, clear to the eye, the massive stampede of thundering, mindless power. He peered forward. The three-pronged rock hillock was still too damn far off. He pointed to it and Karen nodded. "Keep going," he yelled at her as he peeled the pinto away in a wide circle and headed back into the face of the onrushing herd. They were moving with astonishing speed and the ground trembled violently now as he continued to race directly at them. He drew the heavy Sharps rifle from its saddle holster, tucked the stock under one arm. He held his course another few moments and felt the perspiration beading on his forehead. The bison were a towering mass of pounding fury now. He was cutting it as close as he dared. The pinto could outrun the stampeding buffalo, but there was always the chance of a stumble, a misstep. He'd be too flat to find, then, he knew. He swung the pinto in a tight circle and fired the big carbine as he did. He emptied the magazine as he turned; the thundering mass didn't even swerve and Fargo cursed softly. It had been a last-minute desperate effort that had a damn small chance of succeeding, and it had failed. Perhaps a dozen riflemen could have diverted the charging herd. Perhaps.

He bent low in the saddle, sent the pinto racing back. The horse needed no urging, aware of the thundering death that raced behind it. He saw the Conestogas come into view and, beyond them, the rise of the rock hillocks. The first wagon was almost at the hillock, almost rolling into the protection of its high, pronged rock. The second one was still at least a minute away. Sixty seconds to safety and less than that from death. The bison were almost close enough to touch now and Fargo drew the big Colt from its holster. The first wagon was just racing into the three-pronged rise of rock, in through a slight incline of an opening. He turned in the saddle, took aim at one wild, red-rimmed eye, the nearest bison in the mass of stampeding forms. He fired, the only route where the thick skull wouldn't deflect the bullet. He saw the buffalo stumble, pitch forward. Three more following fell over the fallen form and the others swerved to each side. He had gained but a few seconds, but every second was vital now.

He raced up beside the horses, saw they were slowing, their wind gone. A defile appeared in the rocky hillock, a few yards before the main opening where the first wagon had gone. He reached out, grabbed the nearest horse by the cheek strap, and turned the team. Yards were seconds and the stampeding herd was all but upon them. Fargo held on to the horse's strap, raced with the team into the little opening. The first two buffalo grazed the tailgate of the Conestoga as it rolled into the rock sanctuary; Fargo reined up, looked back to watch the stampeding buffalo diverge, splitting in two, a great black-brown river flowing around the rocks. The ground continued to tremble as they thundered past on all sides of the little rock hillock. It seemed they would pound past forever as the massive bodies swept by, but finally the last of them passed and their thunder began to trail off in the distance.

Fargo swung down from the saddle, felt the long deep rush of air escape him. The blond who'd called herself Chrissie clambered down from the wagon. "You did well," he told her. "How old are you?"

"Sixteen," she answered, meeting his eyes boldly.

"I'm seventeen," the other girl said. Fargo watched four others climb down from the wagon, no caps now, their hair flowing, young faces gazing back at him.

"You're all sixteen and seventeen?" Fargo frowned.

"I'm eighteen. I'm the oldest," a tall girl with curly brown hair said. "Millie Harris is the youngest. She's fifteen."

Fargo's mouth drew in and he uttered a soft oath. "Stay with your wagon," he ordered, strode off through an opening in the tall rock formation to where the first Conestoga had pulled up. The fury spiraled inside him as he strode on to where Karen stood beside the wagon. She had seen to it that the row of uniformed figures all had their caps on and pulled down. Fargo swept one arm out as he went past, knocking the caps from the nearest three.

"The goddamn masquerade's over," he shouted as the long hair tumbled down, and he saw Karen Fisher's eyes widen as he bore down on her. His big hand shot out, seized her arm, and he yanked her along with him, almost pulling her off her feet as he strode on around the other side of the rocky pinnacle. He spun her around and she bounced off the side of the rock. "You lying little bitch," he rasped. "You're going to give me the truth now, all of it."

She glowered back at him, but the glower had an edge of fear in it. "It wasn't a lie, not all of it," she muttered.

"Just the most important part," Fargo yelled back. "Girls, everyone of them. You really must be some kind of crazy."

Her lips tightened. "All right, so they're girls," she bit out. "But the rest was true."

"What rest?"

"The part about the fire. The school did burn down. Only it was a girls' school, not a military academy. It was my school. I didn't just teach there," she said.

"Then there's no headmaster in Beulah starting up a new school, either," Fargo snapped back.

"No, but there is someone waiting for me to bring the girls, Mr. Thomas Hubbard," she said.

50

"Who the hell is Thomas Hubbard?" Fargo frowned.

"I met him after the fire. He's from Beulah. He told me how he's been wanting to start a school for young ladies there. He said he'd finance such a school if I'd come to run it and bring the girls as the core. Of course, I jumped at the offer."

"You could've just sent the girls back home," Fargo said.

"I would have had to refund the tuition for every girl and I couldn't do that," Karen Fisher said, peered at the stone in the big man's face. "I didn't have the money. I had no choice but to accept Mr. Hubbard's offer. I couldn't send them back."

"So you decided to get them scalped instead," Fargo clipped out.

Karen's lips tightened again. "No, dammit. I decided to get to Beulah and start over," she flung back.

"By lying, passing them off as boys," Fargo returned.

"Would you have taken the job if you knew they were girls?" she asked quickly, looked smug at the frown in his eyes. "No, you almost refused as it was," she said.

He glowered back. "Where'd you get the damn uniforms."

"A dry-goods salesman's wagon. He'd bought them from a boy's school back east. I decided it might avoid a lot of trouble if the girls were dressed as boys from a military school and I'm sure I was right," she said, her chin lifting.

"Maybe passing through some towns," Fargo snorted. "That explains all that bullshit about the tarpaulins and the boys needing their privacy." She shrugged admission and Fargo's eyes narrowed again in fury. "And now, because of your damnfool ways and lying stories, I'm out here in the middle of the Dakota Territory with a dozen teenage girls," he threw at her. "I ought to fan your little ass so hard you can't sit for a week."

51

She kept her chin up, met his fury. "That will hardly change anything at all, will it?" she said.

"Yes, it would," he growled.

"How?" She frowned.

"It'd make me feel better. I don't like being hornswoggled," he said, took a half-step toward her.

The moment of fright touched her eyes. "All right, I'm sorry I lied to you," she said quickly. "But I had no choice, not about any of it," she said.

"There's always a choice," he said. "You made yours out of stubborn, damnfool self-interest."

"I didn't have the money to return," she insisted. "Mr. Hubbard's offer was a perfect solution."

"For getting all of you dead," Fargo said. He turned away, cursing under his breath. "Get the hell back to your wagon."

"What are you going to do?" she asked.

"Get some sleep, soon as I finish kicking myself for ever having believed you," he said. She walked past, her lips turned in tightly, to disappear around the edge of the tall rocks. Fargo ducked through another small opening in the formation and brought the pinto back, unsaddled the horse, and bedded down behind a length of rock that formed a little box-canyonlike rectangle. The bison wouldn't return, he knew. They'd stampede for perhaps another hour, then slow as the panic dissipated and in time regroup, drift back across the prairie, taking days to do so. He settled down, closed his eyes, not wanting to think about what he'd learned this night. Damn lying little bitch, he muttered silently as he fell asleep.

# 4

The rocks shielded the morning sun from him and he woke later than he'd intended. The little box-canyon area was hot, the new sun already baking stone, and he washed with canteen water, saddled the pinto, and went around to the other side of the rock in boots and trousers only. The wagons had been pulled out onto the flatland, twelve figures, Karen to one side, waiting beside them. No more disguises, he saw, the game over, the girls in shirts and blouses, most still wearing the uniform trousers but a few in riding skirts. His eyes moved across each face, young, clear-eyed, all attractive. Three blonds, five with brown hair, three with jet-black locks, and one redhead. Their eyes stayed on him, curious, even bold, but no fear in any of them. He shook his head, his face hard as the rock behind him, halted at the blond called Chrissie.

"Good morning." She smiled brightly.

"What the hell's good about it?" Fargo growled.

She half-shrugged, dropped the bright smile. She had small high breasts and a narrow waist, her blouse tucked in tightly. His eyes went to the girl beside her, dark-brown curls, cut short, dark eyes, a round, attractive face. He paused at the next one, light-brown hair and hazel eyes, cool amusement in them, a strong chin and nice lips, good shoulders and pillowy breasts under a yellow shirt.

"Do you want me to make introductions?" he heard Karen say.

"I'll do my own introducing if and when," Fargo growled, his eyes going down the line again.

"I told the girls you disapprove of going on," he heard Karen say, and he turned to her.

"Disapprove?" he echoed. "Another schoolteacher word."

"Everyone has voted to go on," Karen said.

"You're all crazy, then," Fargo said.

The blond, Chrissie, spoke up. "It'd take months for most of us to go back home," she said. "Miss Fisher told us that she mightn't have enough money to send us all back. Besides, none of us really want to go home and we know Miss Fisher is trying to do the very best for us."

Fargo glanced at Karen. "Miss Fisher puts out a good story," he said.

"She's in it with us," the brunette called Joannie, answered. "It's not as though she were sending us off on our own. She's risking her neck with us."

Fargo's eyes held on Karen and she met his glance coolly. The lying little bitch had done a good job of selling the package, but Chrissie's one sentence had said even more. They didn't want to go back. It was all an adventure for them and the terrible thing was that they'd no idea of the savage realities that adventure could bring. Karen's voice cut into his thoughts.

"Going back is out of the question for another reason," he heard her say firmly. "Three of the water kegs sprung leaks last night. We're about out of water. There's a line of hills on the horizon to the north. We can probably find water there."

"Maybe. It'll take a day to reach them," he said, and went to the kegs, examined each. Only one held any water, just enough to let them make the hills. "You'll need caulking for these others," he said.

"We have it in the tool locker in the other wagon,"

Chrissie said. "We thought we'd caulk tonight so it can harden overnight."

"If you help us get to the hills and find some water, you can go on your way," Karen said stiffly.

"Miss Fisher, that's not what you promised us," Fargo heard Chrissie protest.

"I never *promised* anything," Karen said quickly.

"But you did," the girl said.

"What did she promise?" Fargo asked Chrissie.

"To try to get you to stay on. We don't want to go on without you with us," the girl said.

Fargo's eyes took on mild surprise and a glint of amusement as he turned them on Karen Fisher.

"I don't beg anyone for anything," she snapped. "Certainly not you."

"Lying beats begging anytime, right?" Fargo slid at her, and saw her eyes narrow.

"I did what I had to do," she returned.

"With your own interests in mind," Fargo tossed at her, and turned to Chrissie. "Get in the wagons. I'll take you to the hills. We'll see about the rest there," he said, turned away from the smile that flashed across the girl's face. Stinking setup, he murmured inwardly as he strode to the pinto. One hard-nosed little bitch and a bunch of wide-eyed kids. He swung onto the pinto, leaving his shirt off. The air had turned still, not a breeze stirring. He waved the wagons on and headed north toward the distant horizon and the barely visible line of hills. Karen came up beside him.

"You could put a shirt on," she remarked stiffly.

"You could take yours off," he said. "It's going to get hotter." She shot a quick glare at him, turned, and rode back to ride alongside the wagons. Fargo increased speed and rode on ahead, his eyes constantly moving back and forth across the plains and scanning the ground until he called a rest at midday. Karen's blouse, soaked with perspiration, clung to the shape of her breasts as if molded there, and she saw his appreciative enjoyment. She climbed onto the front of the first Conestoga.

"I'll only be a minute. I'm going to change my shirt," she told him.

"Too bad. I sort of like it that way," Fargo remarked mildly.

"Is lechery just a built-in part of you?" she said, glaring.

"Yes, ma'am," He grinned. "Honest lechery is a sign of good character."

She vanished into the wagon with another glare and he walked to where two of the girls were sipping from the water keg, using the wooden ladle that hung beside the keg. He saw their eyes travel over the power of his hard-muscled chest, linger on the flowing line of waist and tight stomach muscles, the beauty of his symmetry.

"I'm Katherine," the one said, red-haired with dark-blue eyes, a handful of freckles across the bridge of her nose. She wore her shirt loose, but it didn't hide the deep fullness of her breasts.

"Pam," the other one said, smaller, hazel-eyed with short-cut brown hair and a neat, compact shape, everything proportioned.

"I don't know if I'll ever remember everyone's name," Fargo said. Their eyes held frank approval of what they saw as they looked at him, and he felt the earthy, lusty quality they radiated, the frank eagerness of youth. He took the ladle, sipped slowly from it as Pam reached out, touched the half-moon scar on his forearm.

"What kind of a scar is that?" she asked.

"Bear claw. Grizzly," he said between sips.

"You fought off a grizzly alone?" the red-haired gasped.

"Not my idea, I can tell you that," Fargo said. "I was lucky to get away."

"Will you go on with us?" Katherine asked, and he saw the waiting in their faces, a combination of little-girl pleading and very womanly asking. "Please?"

"We'll never make it alone," Pam said. "Miss Fisher's a very determined person, but I don't think she can get there alone."

"That's damn right," Fargo said as he hung the ladle back on the peg alongside the water keg. Karen stepped from the other Conestoga in a fresh light-blue shirt and he saw her eyes narrow as she took in the girls beside him.

"Back in the wagons, everyone," she ordered, and Pam and Katherine turned away. Fargo watched two of the others climb onto the two extra horses; he walked to the pinto, climbed into the saddle, and waved the wagons forward. He rode out in front and Karen appeared alongside him a few moments later. "I hope you'll remember that these girls are very young and very impressionable," she said stiffly.

"Just like me," he agreed amiably.

She shot a sharp glance at him. "I'm serious. Please watch your manners and your language around them."

"I sure as hell will do that," he said as he cantered off. He rode on, out of sight of the wagons, picked up three old Indian pony trails, and farther on, reined to a halt as he spied another set of tracks. He dismounted, knelt down to study them, was still doing so when Karen rode up.

"Sioux?" she asked at once.

"No Indian ponies. These horses had shoes on," he said.

"What then?"

His eyes read the tracks again. "A good lot of them, moving together but strung out. Buffalo hunters, most likely," he said.

"Then there's no cause for alarm," she said loftily, and Fargo rose to his feet, climbed onto the pinto, and de-

57

cided not to tell her anything about buffalo hunters. The wagons rolled up and he waved them on. "I thought we might get some rest," Karen said. "This heat is draining."

He peered into the distance, the hills still only a thin line. "No rest," he said curtly. "I want to make those hills by sundown and we'll just about do it." He moved on and heard the wagons following. During the rest of the afternoon, he fell back to ride alongside the wagons two or three times. The last time he swung alongside the girls riding the extra horses, peered sharply at them. "Everyone holding up?" he asked.

"Sure," the one said. "I'm Terry." Fargo nodded at the black, shining hair and the eyes to match, broad shoulders and good breasts that bounced in unison as she rode. "This is Barbara," she introduced, gesturing to the other girl, brown hair pulled back in a ponytail, a bright, pretty face with inquisitive eyes and a long, lean horsewoman's figure. "Ride with us awhile so we have something to look at besides the prairie," Terry said.

"Why not?" Fargo agreed. "I kind of like the view back here better myself."

The black-haired girl's smile was full of female wisdom having nothing to do at all with her years.

When they reached the hills, the day was closing down, the sun starting to slide over the horizon line, and Fargo was riding point again. He was glad to see the line of shrub grass at the base of the hills and, rising just beyond it, the dense growth of chickweed. The hills, which could have been only dry-rock rises, held greenery and moisture, and he guided the wagons up a narrow incline that spread out some. In the last minutes of daylight, behind a thick stand of short chokecherry trees, he found a deep stream and pulled the wagons to a halt just below it.

"Get a fire started for yourselves," he told Karen as the others clambered from the wagons. "I'm going to wash off some prairie dust before bedding down." He led the pinto through the chokecherry to the stream, shed his clothes in the last of the light, and sank into the coolness of the water. He let the water course around his legs, just deep enough to cover them, cooling, cleansing, relaxed his body. He'd just finished, stood up, and put on brief shorts to let the air dry the rest of his body, when he saw the two forms come through the thickness of the short trees. They took shape as Chrissie and Pam, and the blond held out her arm as they came up to him.

"We thought you'd like a nice, woolly towel," she said.

"Much obliged." He nodded as he took the towel. As he began to dry himself, he watched the girls take in the power of his thighs, linger on the brief trunks that clung to his crotch.

"Miss Fisher said we should stay away from you," Pam said, a hint of laughter in her voice. "She said you have a bad reputation."

Fargo continued drying himself with their towel and saw their eyes stay on his body. "What kind of bad reputation?" he asked mildly.

"Oh, you know, about drinking and women," Chrissie said airily.

"Honey, that's no bad reputation, that's a good one," Fargo said, and Chrissie's giggle was infectious.

"She said you have no self-discipline," Pam added.

"And she's jealous as hell about that, besides being all wrong," Fargo said, and they giggled again as he handed the towel back. "Thanks, again," he said.

"We'd better get back," Chrissie said, and Fargo watched them hurry away, hips swaying, tight little rears disappearing into the darkness. He went upstream a half-dozen yards and spread out his bedroll, pulled on trousers. He'd just finished when he heard Karen Fisher's voice.

"Fargo?" she called from the darkness.

"Up here," he called back. "Follow the stream."

He heard her moving, waited until she took shape along the bank of the stream. "The girls are insistent you eat with us. Will you?" she asked, moving closer. She'd changed shirts again, this one crisp, laying stiffly against her breasts.

"Just the girls?" he asked.

"I'm happy to have you join us. I told you once, we should share whenever we can on a trip of this nature," she said, unable to keep the stiffness out of her voice.

"You're all heart, honey," Fargo commented.

"Dammit, Fargo, I'm trying to be nice," she flared.

"Try harder," he said.

"You're too used to women throwing themselves at you," she said, sniffing.

"You're too used to lying to yourself and calling it self-discipline," he returned.

She shot a glance of disdain at him. "You're quite impossible."

"Wrong again. I'm possible as hell." He grinned. She spun away, started to stride off, stumbled, would have fallen into the stream if he hadn't caught her arm. "Self-discipline goeth before a fall," he remarked, and she shook his hand away and strode on. He followed casually as she led the way down to the small fire between the two Conestogas. Beans and salt pork cooked together in a kettle smelled delicious and the red-haired Katherine handed him a tin plate heaped high, sat down close beside him. A girl with deep-brown hair and a tight shirt that pressed on pillowy breasts sat down equally close on the other side of him.

"I'm Frances." She smiled warmly and her thigh touched his leg.

Chrissie sat opposite him. "Tell us about being a trailsman," she said.

"I doubt Fargo wants to talk about his life," Karen cut in.

60

"I don't mind," Fargo corrected, catching the flash of disapproval in her eyes. "I do what I want when I want. That's how I like it. I'm my own boss," he said to the others. "It may be dangerous, but it's never dull." He pulled a few tales out of memories for them and then showed Chrissie, Pam, and the redhead how to caulk the water kegs.

"It's time to turn in. It's been a long day," Karen announced.

"We're not tired," the one with the ponytail, Barbara, answered.

"I believe I know what's best for you," Karen told her crisply. "Turn in now." There was a small murmur of discontent, but they began to obey. Fargo rose, saw the black-haired girl, Terry, watching him, in her eyes something he couldn't read, a dark, quiet dancing.

Karen walked to the edge of the fading firelight with him. Her fine-lined features, half-silhouetted in the flickering light, gave her the delicacy of a head on a cameo brooch. "Are you staying on in the morning?" she asked as she halted at the edge of the wagon.

"Not because of anything you've done or your twelve hundred dollars," he told her coldly.

"You've suddenly become a man of principle?" she tossed back. "Or is it pity?"

"Maybe some of both," he said." Or maybe something else."

"What?"

"Maybe I just want to stay around till I find another water trough," he said, saw her lips press onto each other as she spun, pulled herself up onto the wagon, and vanished inside. But not before he'd glimpsed the long, nicely turned length of leg again as her skirt rose up. He smiled as he turned away. Anger was no good for self-discipline.

He returned to where he'd laid out his bedroll upstream and undressed to his trunks and bedded down. He put the

61

big Colt within arm's reach and lay back, watched the moon slowly move across the blue velvet cloth that was the sky. He'd lain perhaps a half-hour when he heard the faint sound, brush being moved aside, too slowly for gopher. He half-turned, listened again, sat up, and heard the half-whispered call, "Fargo?"

"Over here," he said, and the brush moved again, a form appeared, took shape. "Chrissie," he said frowning. "What the hell are you doing here?"

Chrissie came over to him and he saw she wore a flimsy nightdress. She sank down on her knees beside him, a broad, glowing smile on her face. "I won," she breathed.

"You won what?" he asked.

"Coming to you first. We drew straws," she said and, with a quick, sudden gesture, flung the nightdress from her shoulders, let it cascade down to the ground. She flipped onto the bedroll with a quick, half-gasped giggle, and Fargo stared at the lithe beauty of her, narrow-hipped and long-legged, the small high breasts pert and saucy, a young coltish figure. She leaned into him, her eyes dancing.

"Just hold a second," Fargo said. "You mean you all were into drawing straws?"

Chrissie nodded happily. "Everybody. Except Miss Fisher, of course," she said. Her arms went around him and the small high breasts pressed into his chest, firm and throbbing.

"Damn," Fargo murmured. There'd be time for more questions later. Chrissie was a sparkling fountain of eagerness and he pressed his mouth to her lips. She made a little half-giggle and then her mouth opened for him as he pressed her back onto the bedroll. He cupped one high, small breast, smooth as silk, and the tiny nipple hardly raised. His thumb caressed the little pink point and he felt it grow firm, a tiny firmness, and he moved his lips to it.

"Aaah . . . aaah," Chrissie gasped, wriggled her lithe body against him; he caressed the tiny firmness with his tongue and he heard her half-gasp, half-giggle, and her arms grasped his neck, holding him hard against her breast. He felt the little pink tip lift, harden yet hardly raised above the soft curve of her areola, a tight little pink circle. Chrissie moved again against him, pressing, seeking, the lithe young-colt body half-twisting over his—wanting, yet unsure of how or when—and he ran his hand down over the inside of her thigh and felt her pelvis twist back, lay flat, little tremors moving through her legs. "Oh, oh, ooooh . . ." The sounds came from her in short, broken-breath gasps and he moved his hand up to the dark tangle of her and now the little tremors grew stronger. He pressed his hand down on her little mound and she cried out, a sound of delight flung out into the night. He kept his hand there and paused, let himself take in the lean beauty of her, sweet wanting eagerness, her hands fluttering over his chest, down to his abdomen, down farther, then quickly moving away, unsure, uncertain, and full of wanting. The brief trunks had left his hips and he caught her hand, pulled it down to him. "Aaaaiiiii . . ." she cried out as he held her hand against him, but there was no more pulling away and her fingers wrapped around his maleness with a fierce possessiveness.

His moved through the small, black bushiness and against the moist warmth of her, and her groan came first, turned into quick excited breaths, and she clasped her legs together, holding his hand there, crying out little sounds as he explored, opened, pressed. "Yes, oh, God, oh, God," she murmured, repeating the words in a rhythmn that began to match the little tremors coursing through her body. She cried out, a hint of pain masked by anxious wanting, as he probed, brought himself over her, and slowly touched her, holding the very tip of his gift at her. He moved slowly, sliding forward carefully, and he felt

63

the long, lean thighs falling against his sides, upraised, knees pressing into his ribs. She was making tiny urging sounds mixed with long, low gasps, and then, suddenly, the tremors became a violent shaking and he discarded gentleness, plunged forward.

"Eeeeiiiaaa . . ." she screamed out, pushed back from him for a brief moment, then came pushing hard against him with the violent, electric shaking, as though a bolt of lightning had suddenly set her afire. "Fargo, Fargo, Fargo," she cried out as her lips sought his and he let his mouth crush hard against her. "Yes, yes, please, I want, I want . . ." she murmured, and she was trembling like a leaf in a terrible storm. He slid back, almost out of her, and she screamed in protest but he held there as suddenly her legs grew taut, lifted, her heels digging into the ground. He pressed forward at once as she exploded, her mouth pressed against his shoulder muffling the scream that came from her. He held her in her moment of total ecstasy, held her tight against him as she throbbed violently, felt her body shudder, finally begin to relax, and he lowered her to the ground, staying inside her.

Chrissie's arms clung to him and her knees continued to press into his sides until, abruptly, they fell away and he watched the tremors slowly leave her. "Oh," she murmured. "Oh, God. Oh, wow." He tried to move back, but her arms held him until, finally, he slowly drew from her and she uttered a whimper, then relaxed her arms as he pulled himself onto one elbow to look down at her. Her eyes were fastened on him, full of brightness, her lips slightly parted, and she lay there, just gazing at him like a wood sprite caught in a relaxed moment.

She gave a little sigh. "Too quick," she murmured but without complaint. "I guess it's always that way the first time, too much, too quick. You're not ready for it."

"I guess so," Fargo said, and tried remembering what it was like the first time, decided there'd been too many times since then for remembering. Chrissie half-turned, reached up, took his head, and pressed it down onto one high, young breast; he opened his lips, took all of it into his mouth, and felt the tremor course through her body instantly.

"Oh, yes . . . yes, yes," she breathed, and her hips began to move at once and she turned to press her soft little pubic mound tight against him. He moved, rested his organ against the very edge of her, and a little squeal of pleasure came from her and suddenly her breathing had become short, full of gasped sounds. He felt her lithe legs move, lift, try to open her warmth for him, but he made her wait, let her twist and turn and felt her wanting grow. Her hands pulled at his back. "Please, Fargo, oh, gosh, please," she murmured, and as he rose, moved with her, entered the wet waiting of her, she was trembling eagerly and pressing her breasts up for his mouth. "Oh, my, oh, my God, oh," Chrissie cried with his every slow movement, and her gasps had the quality of pure joyful exuberance; this time he moved more quickly for her as her knees pressed hard into his ribs, her legs half-encircling, falling away, moving aimlessly, and he felt the learning, trying newness of her every movement. He moved into her with increasing power and suddenly her body began to shake and once again her scream was held muffled against his chest as she clung to him, shaking violently. Finally, after seconds that were not seconds at all but timeless moments in space, she drew her head back and he felt her arms relax and he let her lower herself back down on the bedroll. "Oh, wow," she breathed, staring up at him as he stroked the high, small breasts gently.

He waited, let her breath return, lay on one elbow beside her. "Let's talk some," he said. "About drawing straws."

Her little half-giggle came at once. "We just decided,"

she said, rising up to rest on both elbows, stretching the young wood-sprite body.

"You just decided? All of you, just like that?" he questioned.

"More or less," Chrissie said. "I guess it was a lot of different things all building up."

"Such as?"

"We're all young, healthy, wanting. There were some boys near the school. They came to dances. Some of us managed to sneak away from Miss Fisher, but there was never the time or place for anything much. Besides, they were only boys." She ended the sentence with disdain beyond her years, thought for a moment as her eyes stayed on Fargo. "And there was something else," she said. "We know this trip is dangerous. We know we maybe mightn't make it and we decided we ought to do it at least once while we could. It just seemed it'd be terrible to die without having lived. We figured we owed that to ourselves. So when you rode in that morning and rescued us, and Miss Fisher, from those men, I guess everyone's secret dreams and fantasies came alive."

"Secret dreams and fantasies?"

"Sure, all girls have secret dreams and fantasies. We all dream about a perfect lover coming out of the blue. When you joined us, it seemed all our secret dreams might come real, only not real enough, so we decided to do something about that."

"I'll be dammed," Fargo muttered, studied Chrissie's young face, too open for anything but truth. He cupped one little firm breast in his hand. "Was it worth all those secret dreams?"

"Was it ever." She giggled and flung her arms around him. Her sheer exuberance, unstudied open joy, was fresh as a mountain waterfall. "I have to get back," she said, pulling away and in one quick movement tossing the

66

nightdress over herself. "You going to go to sleep now?" she asked, eyeing him sideways.

He smiled. "You asking if I've any energy left?"

She laughed, nodded as she stood up. "I guess so."

"Enough," he told her. "You thinking of coming back?"

"No, we made a rule about that," Chrissie said, turning to leave. "Good night, Fargo," she called back happily.

"Sleep well, Chrissie," he said, watched her vanish into the dark of the trees. He lay back and made a small wager with himself. The moon slowly rose higher in the sparkled sky and he was beginning to think he'd lost the wager when he heard the rustle of leaves, hesitant sounds, cautious and uncertain. "This way," he called softly, sat up, and watched the figure come into view. He saw the shirt first, dim yellow in the moonlight, long bare legs below the tail of it. Frances of the yellow shirt and the pillowy breasts, he murmured inwardly. His wager with himself hadn't been on who, only that he'd have another visitor.

Frances came toward him, dropped to her knees on the bedroll beside him. She'd none of Chrissie's bubbling, coltish eagerness, her face unsmiling, almost grave. He watched as her eyes traveled over him, slowing at the bulge in his briefs, moving to his face, meeting his glance. Her face remained unsmiling, her lips pressed tightly together. He reached out, touched her cheek gently with the back of his hand. "You don't have to stay, Frances," he said. "Maybe you've had second thoughts?"

She shook her head slowly. "No. I want to stay," she said very softly. She sounded terribly little girl, but in her face, suddenly, there was more, a deep-eyed restlessness. He lowered his hand, began to unbutton the yellow shirt. She didn't move as he undid the top button, then the next, went down to the others. Her face remained unsmiling, her eyes on his as he opened the last button, pushed the shirt from her shoulders. The pillowy breasts came fully into view, very womanly for a girl so young, wide with softly curving undersides and surprisingly large, dark-pink areolas surrounding the light-pink flat tips. Her waist was fuller than Chrissie's, her hips wider, a completely different figure already nudging womanliness, a different kind of beauty but still beauty.

He reached out slowly, took both softly firm breasts in his hands, and gently pulled. The sound seemed to come from somewhere inside her abdomen, a tremendous, exploding groan-gasp of air. "Aaaaaaooooooh . . ." she cried, the sound rising, taking on sudden strength, and then, unexpected abruptness, she flung herself forward, wrapping arms around him, her mouth crushing against his. He fell back onto the bedroll, taking her with him, and she half-rolled over, the gasping, groaning sounds still coming from her. He buried his head into the large, pillowy breasts and heard her cry out, twist, pushing her breasts upward to find his mouth. "Oh, oooooh, oh, I love it, I love it," she gasped as he caressed her breasts with his lips, drawing little circles around the large areolas with his tongue. Frances' body moved half under him, her legs drawing up and stretching out again, and he let his hand move across the full-figured beauty of her. She was half-groaning as he reached the black patch, larger and denser by far than Chrissie's, the mound fuller, thicker. She freed a hand from against his body, reached down, seized his fingers, and pressed them tightly between her legs. "Aaa-aaggghhh . . ." she exploded, a rasping sound, clasping his hand between her thighs. He pushed his hand down deeper between the soft, young flesh of her thighs and she arched her back but her legs closed around him. "Yes, yes," she whispered, and he made his hand into a fist, pushed it deeper, and suddenly her thighs came open, her back arched again, and her hips began to pump up and down. He came over her, plunged quickly, and she screamed in glory, screamed again, and he felt her legs moving up and down, first one then the other, a wild throbbing in her, and gasped words became just sounds run together, sounds of wanting and waking, ecstasy and fulfillment.

The gasped groan rose again as her moment came, tearing out of some deep, dark place inside her, a frenzied animal-like quality to it, and she locked herself around him with her arms, her legs entwined around his calves until the whirling, wild ecstasy left her and she moved to wrap herself against him, wanting the embers of his warmth. She lay still, very still, and he stroked her back, leaned over her, and caressed the soft pillowy breasts. He met her eyes, deep and dark, peering at him, her face still unsmiling. "Was I all right?" she asked. "For a beginner?"

"Is that so important to you?" he asked gently. "Nobody's in a contest."

"Was I all right?" she asked again.

"You were fine." He smiled. "For a beginner."

Her eyes held his and slowly she smiled, putting youth into her face, youth and a sudden surge of womanly satisfaction. "Thanks," she said simply. "It was important to me. It's a problem of mine. I'm always afraid people won't think well of me."

"I think very well of you," Fargo said. Frances reached up, kissed him, her lips tender.

"I was afraid," she said. "I wanted to come so much, but I was afraid." She looked at him closely. "But you knew that, of course."

"I had an idea," he said, and she sat up, reached for the yellow shirt.

"I wish I could stay, but I can't. We have to be careful. Miss Fisher makes rounds some nights," Frances said. He rose with her, held her against him for a moment more. "There's so much more to do, to learn, isn't there?" she said.

"All in time," he told her, rubbed his hand over the smooth nakedness of her bottom under the tail of the yellow shirt. Her small smile held womanly wisdom in it and he watched her turn, start to hurry off. She paused at the edge of the trees.

"You can go to sleep now," she called back, and disappeared into the darkness. Fargo shook out his bedroll, lay down on it, and pulled the blanket over himself. The trip had taken on unexpected rewards. Damn, he murmured to himself. He wasn't one for surprises. They usually came up unpleasant. But this was sure one damn exception. He rolled over and slept soundly.

He woke to the sounds of splashing water and high-pitched shouts of laughter. He lay still for a moment, listening, then rose, dressed slowly, and found himself still thinking about the night that had brought pleasure and promise. Finished dressing, he gazed out across the flat prairieland, let his eyes move along the line of the hills. When the splashing and shouting stopped, he made his way to the wagons.

Chrissie was holding the reins of the first Conestoga, Pam with the short brown hair on the second, the others all preparing to move out. Karen stood beside the thick-bodied bay and Joannie offered him a tin cup of coffee. He took it, sipped the hot brew, and saw Chrissie smile brightly at him in her usual manner. His eyes found Frances, the yellow shirt easy to spot. She was climbing into the second wagon, chatting with the black-haired Terry. They were good little actresses, all of them, going about with the new day as if there'd been no night, no new dimension added to the trip. He finished the coffee, handed the tin cup back to Joannie, and swung onto the pinto. He waved a hand and the wagons began to roll, following him down to the flatland.

Karen came up alongside him on the bay. "We'll travel on the plains but stay close to the hills," he said.

"Instead of straight across the prairie?" She frowned. "That'll add miles," she said as he nodded.

"Some," he admitted. "But it'll keep us near water and make for better camping at night."

She accepted the answer, but her frown stayed. She kept up with him as he cantered on.

"Beautiful morning, isn't it?" he said. "Bright as a new penny."

"Rather hot for this early, I'd say," she answered.

"Sun's good for you," he beamed. He whistled softly, hummed a few minutes, then lifted his voice, a deep base-baritone.

> My boots are in the stirrups
> And my rope is at my side,
> Show me a spotted pony I can't ride,
> Singing ki-yi, yippi yappi yay. . . .

"You're terribly cheerful this morning," Karen cut in, eyeing him warily.

"Be of good cheer, thy sins shall be forgiven thee." Fargo beamed. "That's what the Good Book says."

"How comforting," she said tartly. "I imagine you ought to be cheerful a good deal more, then."

"Some mornings are easier than others," he said with a wide smile, and cantered on, felt her frown following him. The hills curved slowly northwest and, she was right of course, added extra miles to the journey. But camping on the flat prairie was out of the question now, and he smiled quietly to himself. He found more tracks which told him that the buffalo hunters were moving back and forth over a wide area, splitting into two groups, then joining together again. One set of tracks led to the edge of the hills, he noted with displeasure. During a brief rest at midday, Karen sauntered to where he stood by the pinto.

"We're making good time," he said happily.

Her eyes continued to regard him with wary skepticism. "You've certainly had an abrupt change in attitude," she

72

said thoughtfully. "Frankly, I don't understand it, and anything I don't understand bothers me."

"You must be bothered a lot." He smiled at her and watched her eyes narrow for an instant. "I just decided to make the best of a bad situation. It's called self-discipline," he said, and laughed as she spun on her heel and stalked back to the bay.

An hour before sundown, he led the wagons back into the hills, found an underground spring feeding clear water into a little sinkhole, and had the wagons camp around it. "I'll bed down up there beyond that stand of shadbrush," he announced, pointing to a spot a good twenty-five yards up the hillside.

"I do appreciate the way you've respected the girls' privacy," Karen said, her eyes sincere.

"Wouldn't have it any other way," he said cheerfully, and tossed her a happy smile.

"Stew's ready," he heard Barbara call out, and he sat down with the others to a bowl of dried-beef stew with turnips, finished quickly, and rose to stretch.

"I'll be bedding down now," he said. "Good night." A chorus of good nights followed him and he caught Chrissie's little giggle, smiled quietly as he walked up the hillside and through the shadbush, found a little hollow, and bedded down at once, stripping to his briefs. The nights continued to stay warm and he relaxed, half-dozed. It'd take the camp a while to settle down, he knew. He was almost hard asleep when his cat's ears caught the sound, a twig snapping under a foot. He came awake instantly, listened, heard another footstep at the far edge of the shadbush. "This way," he called softly, turned, and waited until he glimpsed the figure. It neared, became shiny black hair and black eyes, a thin nightgown over deep breasts, clinging to full hips. "Hello, Terry," he said.

The girl came to him, halted, looked down at him, and he watched her eyes move over the powerful beauty of his body, return to his face. "Did you wonder who it would be tonight?" she asked, her voice husky.

"Yes," he admitted, and she half-smiled, sank down beside him. The thin nightgown pressed tight against her breasts, round, full breasts with the nipples standing out clearly. Her eyes went down to his thighs again, held there, finally lifting to meet his own.

"I saw pictures in an old book once, a book I wasn't supposed to see," she began slowly. "It belonged to my father. He teaches history back east. It showed how, in ancient Greece, the man's organ was a sacred symbol. They even had a special God devoted to it, Priapus."

"Those old Greeks had a lot of good ideas," Fargo commented.

"It showed pictures of monuments to the male organ and pictures of women worshiping and making love to it," she said, paused, drew a deep breath. "Ever since I saw them, I've wanted to do that," she said, her voice low. "Crazy, isn't it? My own fantasies," she added.

"No," Fargo told her. "Things haven't changed all that much. I think maybe those old Greeks were just more open about it." He saw the waiting in her black eyes, questions she didn't find words to ask directly, yet she had asked in her own way. He reached down, pushed his trunks from his hips, keeping his eyes on her, lay back on the bedroll. Slowly, she took her eyes from his, looked down across his muscular form.

"Oh, Jesus," he heard her gasp out. "Oh . . . oooooh." She fell forward, across his hips, and little cooing sounds came from her; he felt her hands curl around his organ, caressing, stroking, pressing it to her cheek. "Jesus . . . oh, oh, God," she murmured, her lips moving up and down the sides of his penis, kissing, tracing little lines of wanting. Her tongue touched the tip and then drew away, and he felt her body beginning to writhe atop his hips. Her tongue touched again, tentative, uncertain, wanting in the way of knowing. He moved, slid out from under her, and she cried out at once," No," reached for him again. He swung around to face her, gently opened her lips, showed her how to take him, and her cry became ecstasy as he moved with her and he lay back again and now she understood and wanted and made tiny soft sounds as she pressed and pulled, caressed and held.

He let her go on as long as she wanted and felt himself throbbing with the eagerness of her lips, the exploring joy of her desire, and he held back until finally she lifted her head to his, her legs moving slowly up and down in the eternal invitation. He went to her quickly, sliding into the waiting dark moistness of her and she was quick to move with him in a long, slow rhythm that grew stronger, harsher. No frenzied movement from Terry, everything sensuously drawn out, long, slow writhings while her hands rubbed up and down his ribs. He felt her writhings increase and suddenly she was thrusting hard up against him, taking all of him into her. "Ah . . . ah . . . ah, ah . . ." The sounds came from her in rising crescendo and the lingering cry erupted from her as her instant engulfed her. "Fargo, Fargo . . . oh, please," she called out as though he could make the instant stay. She held hard against him and slowly, reluctantly, fell back, a long-drawn breath escaping her. She clasped his face with her hands, held him against her, and he let her cling until she took her hands away, nestled him against her. He felt one hand reach down, curl around his still-vibrant organ, and the tiny shudder of pleasure that coursed through her.

"They were right, those ancient Greeks," she murmured. "I guessed they were, but I had to know for myself."

"You happy now?" he asked.

"If you can call having one spoon of ice cream being happy," she answered.

"It's a long trip," Fargo remarked, and her smile held

promise. Her fingers caressed, moving gently, and he felt her hand move along the line of his thighs, down again to his organ, around the curve of his testicles, and up along his pelvis, and he realized she was tracing a drawing for her mind to keep.

"I have to go," she said finally. "God, I don't want to, but we made an agreement." She slipped into the nightgown, pressed both hands to him once again, and then hurried away, not looking back, carrying off fantasies made real. Fargo stretched out, closed his eyes, and waited. It was a short wait, the footsteps coming quickly, almost running. He sat up and saw the ponytail tossing.

"Barbara," he called, and she hurried toward him, a rain slicker wrapped around the lithe horsewoman's figure. She flung the slicker away, almost dived into his arms, and pressed herself tight against him, and he felt the trembling of her.

"Quick," he heard her whisper. "Don't let me think. Don't give me time for second thoughts." She kept clinging against him, arms locked around him, fought to stay there as he tried to push her away. "Don't listen to me," she whispered fiercely. "Make me, just make me."

He got his arm up against her ribs, pressed, and she had to let go of her grip; he seized her shoulders, pressed her down on the bedroll, saw her lips open in a gasp. Firm, neat little breasts poked upward, their centers deep pink, the waist below narrow, hips lean and angular, and her legs on the thin side. She drew her knees up, tried to push him away, and he used his thigh to force them aside. He bent his head down, took one deep-pink tip in his mouth, and her arms pushed against him. "No," she whispered. "No, don't, oh, no." He drew all of the firm breast into his mouth and the words became a whispering cry.

"No?" he murmured as his tongue circled the little point.

"No," she whispered hoarsely, "No." And she pushed

upward against him. His hand moved quickly down to her legs and she immediately tried to draw her knees up again. He pushed his hand down farther, pressed her thighs open, and swung over her. "No, no," she cried out, and her hands became fists; beat against his back. He lay for a moment atop her and her struggling halted and he heard the shallow harsh breathing of her. He pressed his mouth over hers and her tongue darted out to meet his and her fists opened, hands pressing against him. He half-rose, thrust forward quickly. "Aaaaiiieee . . ." she screamed. "Aaaaah . . ." She tried to twist away, tore her mouth from his. "No, no, no," she cried out as he held still inside her. He moved slowly, slipping deeper, pulling back a fraction, moving forward again. "Oooooh," she gasped. "Oh, no, no."

"No?" he echoed again, moving gently, then thrusting forward.

"No," she half-screamed, and he thrust again, once again. "No. No, oh, oh, oh, yes . . . yes, oh, yes," she breathed. He stayed with her, felt her arms close around him, holding tight to him, and she came quickly, little screams preceding the final shuddering scream, and she stiffened under him, only the warm, wet muscles contracting on their own, willing their own pleasures, obeying their own impulses only.

Her arms stayed around his neck as she lay back, drawing in harsh, long breaths, and her eyes peered at him, blinked, slowly returned to focused consciousness. A tiny smile touched the corners of her mouth. "Thanks for not listening to me," she said.

"I never listen to words," he said. "Not at times like that."

"It's terrible to want something so much and yet be afraid to want it," she said.

"You still afraid?" he asked.

"No, not anymore," she said, the ponytail tossing.

"Then let's do it right," he said.

"Yes," she murmured. "Oh, yes." Her arms slid around his neck at once, no trembling tension this time, and he explored the angular, lean horsewoman's body, full of young wanting, and this time she was all giving, all eager desire, her final scream a cry of victory. When it was time for her to go back down the hillside, she held him a moment longer before throwing the rain slicker over herself, her eyes wide. "Are we going to make it to Beulah?" she asked. "Tell me the truth. Can we make it?"

"With a little luck," he answered.

"Good," she said with a snort of satisfaction. "I wouldn't want the new me to go to waste."

She swirled the slicker over herself and bounded off to vanish like a young doe in the forest. Fargo went to sleep quickly. The girl's last question had been like tossing a rotten carcass into the middle of a twelve-course banquet and he refused to think about it. He slept soundly till the new day and heard the sounds from the campsite below as he dressed.

Joannie had coffee waiting for him when he wandered down, and he exchanged quick glances with Terry, her black eyes sparkling. He led the wagons onto the prairie a few minutes later and continued to move along the line of the hills. Travois marks held his eyes later in the day, a party of six squaws and three braves, he decided. The marks, at least a day old, went on toward the distant hills to the north and posed no threat. He maintained a steady pace that ate away the day and by nightfall he was on his bedroll in a grassy knoll downwind from where he had camped the wagons.

Joannie appeared first when the night grew still, a girl with limited passion, he decided, willing and wanting but with none of Chrissie's joyful exuberance or Terry's sensuousness. Susan followed her, a girl he had seen only as a peripheral figure, who stayed mostly inside the wagon.

Small, dark-haired, she brought a wire-thin energy, every-thing quick and edged, her lovemaking made of little sur-prises, sudden bursts of passion, and unexpected quietness.

Lying alone, later, he reflected how they were all so different, the same only in their youth, different in body and in spirit, as different in the shape of their breasts as in the shape of their emotions. But the trip was turning out to be a banquet of the sensual and he was enjoying every bite. Karen continued to eye his cheerfulness with suspi-cion and he almost felt grateful to her. It had been her stubborn, self-serving lies that had brought them all out here in the middle of the Dakota Territory but also brought on the private feast of pleasure he was enjoying. The next night he camped the wagons higher in the hills, in a hollow of basalt rock forms hidden away from the prairie below. He made his own campsite farther on in a small boxlike area between the basalt rock, a lone path bisected by tough scrub brush leading to it.

The night turned cool and he made a small fire with dry, sun-baked wood, and the little area turned warm quickly as he stripped to his trunks, lay down on the bed-roll. The tiny fire sent glowing light to dance off the rocks and he was waiting, his ears tuned, as he caught the soft footsteps, the sound of a pebble being dislodged. "Here," he called out. "Go through the scrub brush." The figure emerged from the narrow passageway in moments and he saw the firelight glinting on the long red hair at once. He watched her come toward him, barefoot, wearing a cotton robe held together with a belt.

"Hello, Katherine," he said softly, and the girl came to the edge of the bedroll, halted. A faint red flush in her cheeks didn't come from the firelight's glow and Fargo's eyes took in her straight, tall figure, the high cheekbones giving her face sharp, angled planes, a wide mouth and a long, graceful neck against the red tresses. She was definitely the most beautiful of them all, he decided as she stood unmoving, her eyes boring into his. He rose from the bedroll, took a single step to her, and she remained motionless.

He reached out, undid the belt, and the robe fell open to reveal long, pear-shaped breasts, a narrowed waist that went into full, womanly hips, a convex little tummy, and a dense triangle of dark auburn. She stood unmoving, let him slip the robe from her shoulders. As it fell to the ground, her arms came up, slid around his neck, and her lips opened. She took a half-step and pressed herself against him, her body all warm softness, and her tongue was in his mouth, seeking, asking. He sank down on the bedroll with her and she stayed against him, and his hands found the long, pear-shaped breasts, caressed the points standing high already. He felt her stomach rubbing against his and her legs began to move up and down across his body. Her mouth worked feverishly on his, her tongue a stabbing darting instrument now, and her hand reached out, pulled his hand down to the auburn tangle, and she rolled onto her back, pulling him with her. Soft, gasping breaths came from her but no other sound as he touched the deep secret place, and her legs fell open wide, the eternal beckoning, and there was still no sound but the soft little breaths. Her hips lifted for him, raised upward to welcome his first penetration, and her arms tightened. her fingers digging into his back, and he felt the tiny trickle of blood on his skin. She pumped upward, meeting his slow thrusting, quickened her pace with him, and still there was only the soft, gasped breathing from her, no words, no sounds, no moans.

But there was no lack of passion as her red locks tossed from side to side and she pushed violently up against him. She wrapped her legs over his buttocks and with each pumping, thrusting meeting her nails dug deeper into his back and a fervent wildness took hold of her. But the silence remained and it became a strange almost soundless conjoining, a silent tableau, ecstasy gone mute. Her shaking, pumping pelvis demanded, a passionate petition, and he obeyed happily when he felt her legs straighten, grow rigid. Her hands dug into him and he watched her lips draw back and the silence ended as she laughed, a deep, throaty laugh, and the laugh became a wondrous cry of pleasure and she was smiling, calling out. "Oh, yes, yes, I love, I love, oh, how good, how good," she sang out as he felt her muscles contract, the climax upon her, seizing hold of her, and he came with her as the flaming hair whipped across his face. "Ooooh, how good, good, oh, yes, nice, nice, oh . . . ooh, Fargo," she called out, a singsong cry, a sweet paean of pleasure. The dam of silence had burst and now little happy sounds came from her, almost laughter, deep pleasure sounds, and her hands pulled his head down into the pear-shaped breasts as she sank down, her legs relaxing.

She caressed his head, pressed his face against her, and the happiness was a tangible thing he could almost touch. "I was thinking you'd lost your voice," he said, looking down at the beauty of the high-cheekboned face.

"It was lost," she said. "Lost in the wild wanting inside me."

"You're a beautiful girl, Katherine," he told her, stroking the red hair from her face. "It oughtn't to be wasted in a school stuck out in Beulah."

"I'll only stay the year," she said. "Then I'll go back east. Unless you tell me where you'll be."

He laughed softly. "I could better tell you where the wind will be," he said.

She sat up, her smile almost dreamy. "Then I'll have to make next time even better than this," she said. "Besides, Miss Fisher said the gentleman who's setting up the new school, Mr. Hubbard, spoke of having a boy's school along with it."

"So you're thinking it won't be a dry creek." Fargo laughed and her wise little smile answered. She pulled the robe over, slipped into it, and he stood up with her.

"But I'm planning on a next time with you before that," she said, kissing his cheek, and strode away, looking beautiful even in the bulky robe. He smiled to himself, lay down, reached out to stir the fire that had almost gone out, put another small twig on it. The warmth rushed over him at once as the fire renewed itself and he lay back and wondered who'd be his next visitor. Guessing had become fun of itself. There weren't all that many left. Pam with her short-cut brown hair, Laurie with the doe eyes, Millie Harris, the youngest of all, and he had uncertain thoughts about her, plus Doris and Alice, both quiet-in-the-background types with whom he'd hardly exchanged two words. He lay with his arms behind his head, clad only in the tight, brief trunks, watched the moon above. He half-dozed, woke, realized that no one had appeared, and found himself wondering what had delayed his next visitor. He leaned over, had just finished stirring the little fire, when he heard the footsteps, no quiet, cautious movements but strong, quick sounds. He heard the scrub brush being flung aside.

"Fargo," he heard the voice call out. "Fargo, you bastard. Where are you?"

He felt his lips purse. There was no mistaking the voice. School was over, he murmured silently. "Over here," he called, and rose to his feet.

She came storming through the little passage, halted, her eyes blazing, swept up and down his near-naked form. "All ready and waiting, aren't you?" she flung at him. "Well, there's nobody else coming, you rotten bastard. You animal, you . . . you lecher!"

"Flattery isn't going to get you anywhere," he said mildly.

She came toward him, fury in her face. "Don't make

jokes with me," she spit. "Taking advantage of those young girls. How could you?"

"I don't think you know those girls very well," he said calmly.

"I know them and I know just what happened. It was your influence," she said.

"It was all their idea," he countered.

"You could have turned them down. You could have said no," she snapped furiously.

"I'm crazy to have come out here with you, but I'm not that crazy," he said.

"Of course not, you couldn't do the decent thing, the honorable thing. All you saw was a chance to play rooster in a barnyard."

"Try cock," he murmured.

"Haven't you any morals? Haven't you any principles at all?" she threw at him. "I tried to teach these girls decency and proper behavior."

"Oh, they behaved right proper, all of them," he said.

Her eyes raged at him. "This explains why you were so damn cheerful all of a sudden," she shouted.

"Now, didn't you say we ought to share on a trip like this?" he asked mildly. "The girls and me, we've just been doing a little sharing."

"Rotten, amoral, unprincipled bastard," she shot back.

"Tell me, honey, are you so all-fired mad because they didn't include you? Because you didn't get to draw a straw?" he slid at her. Her hand came up in a wide arc and he easily ducked away from the swing. His eyes darkened and his voice took on an edge. "Any one of them is a lot more woman than you are," he threw at her. "They don't lie to themselves about their own feelings and call it self-discipline."

She flew at him, tried to rake his face with her nails. "Rotten, rotten," she cried, her voice choking. "Bastard."

She clawed at him again and he ducked aside, caught her arm, spun her around.

"Damn little hellcat, aren't you?" he said with some surprise.

She tried to free herself, aimed a kick at his shin he just managed to avoid. "Son of a bitch," she hissed.

"Such language, Miss Fisher," he said.

She brought her knee up, aimed at his crotch. He avoided the maneuver, twisted her arm back. "Goddamn you . . . owooo," she gasped.

"Knock it off and you won't get hurt," he told her. She was starting to scream at him when his ears picked up the other sound. His eyes turned to ice at once and clapped a hand over her mouth, held it there. "Shut up, damn you," he hissed. She stopped struggling at the tone in his voice, but he kept his hand over her mouth as he strained his ears to listen. The sound neared, horses pounding along the plains, slowing down. He saw Karen's eyes grow wide and the fear come into them and he took his hand from her mouth, stepped to the side of the basalt to listen.

"Sioux?" she whispered.

He didn't answer, his ears straining, and he picked up the sound again. They were moving on. He turned to her. "No, these horses had shoes. Buffalo hunters," he said. "I don't know what they heard, you and your goddamn shouting. Sounds carry a hell of a ways out here, especially at night." His hand snapped out, caught her by the neck of the gray dress, his voice a tight, whispered rasp. "Get the hell down to the others. Tell them to stay quiet as mice for the rest of the night. You hear me? No talking, no arguing, nothing but silence."

She nodded and he sent her on her way with a hard shove, watched her stumbling through the passage and disappear. He kicked dirt over the fire, dousing it, and lay down on the bedroll. The riders had heard something and had ridden out to investigate. Luckily, the rocks shielded

84

any direct glow from the fire and hid the wagons. For now. They might return to look around some more come daylight. He'd have to be careful in the morning. He turned on his side, thoughts of pleasure pushed aside by danger, drew sleep to himself.

He was awake at dawn, moving carefully along the edge of the basalt rocks to a place where he could see out over the prairie. The rising sun spread across the plains like a yellow tablecloth slowly being unfolded. Gophers and jackrabbits stirred and, in the distance, a pronghorn antelope bounded off with effortless ease. His lips stayed a harsh line as he scanned the prairie again. They weren't camped out nearby on the plains, but that didn't mean a great deal. They could be somewhere else too near. He turned, made his way down to the wagons. The girls were just emerging, some in slips only, rinsing their faces. Terry, in only a half-slip, made no effort to put a blouse on as he appeared; he saw Karen to one side, in a loose robe, surprise and angry disapproval in her eyes as she stared at the girl. Terry casually reached for her blouse, wriggled into it, her deep breasts making delicious little motions.

Fargo beckoned to Karen and she came forward, her chin high, eyes full of sharp defiance. The others moved to form a semicircle around him. "I'm going out looking," he said, his voice low. "You stay here. Whatever you do, do it quietly. I don't want any noise."

"Why all this fuss about some buffalo hunters?" Karen asked icily. "Or is this just your way of trying to draw attention from what's been going on around here, your own little diversion?"

She saw the blue ice form in his eyes. "You've a real talent for being wrong," he told her, and her lips grew tight. "Let me tell you about buffalo hunters, Miss Schoolteacher. They're not a bunch of ordinary cowhands out for a hunt. They're a special breed. They're mostly renegades—mean, rough-and-tough men who don't care about anything or anybody. The Indian hunts buffalo for food and for clothing. He uses every part of the buffalo—fur, skin, bones, horns, and meat. He wastes nothing and only kills enough to meet his needs. The buffalo hunters kill everything in sight—bulls, cows, and calves. They take only the fur and leave the rest for the buzzards. They enjoy wiping out whole herds. They don't give a damn if there's a buffalo left standing in the whole land so long as they get their furs. They're men who don't give a damn about anything and they'd just love to find this little harem out here in the middle of noplace."

He spun, swung up onto the pinto, and fastened Karen with another hard look. "That answer you about the fuss over the nice buffalo hunters?" he speared. He saw her glance away, look at the girls, look away again, and he turned the pinto and started to move down toward the bottom of the hills. He rode along the edge of the hills, his eyes searching the ground. He'd gone almost a mile when he saw the tracks leading into the hills from the prairie, vanishing quickly on the rocky floor of the region. They'd ridden into the hills during the night and he found a hoofprint here and there, another farther along. He rode slowly, carefully, up deeper into the hills, through green brush, hill grass, and some chickweed as the rocky underfooting turned to soil. He picked up their tracks again, fresher, at least three or four horses, perhaps more.

He found the place where they'd camped for the night, his eyes hardening at the way they'd left the site. Their tracks led back higher in the hills and he followed them, an uneasy feeling gathering in the pit of his stomach. When he saw the tracks begin to move downward, the uneasy feeling became bitter apprehension. He continued pursuing the tracks, cursing under his breath as they led downward. When the two Conestoga wagons came into sight, he swung from the pinto, his lips drawn back as he surveyed the scene. The four men, spread out, faced the girls, who were gathered against the first wagon, Karen standing in front of them. Fargo worked his way on foot down a narrow defile of rock, emerged to glance again at the scene just below him. Nothing had changed, but he could hear voices now. It was plain what had happened. the buffalo hunters had ridden into the hills, camped, then doubled back higher up. It was certain they'd glimpsed the two wagons when they neared the site.

Fargo, sliding along on his rump, moved down a steep face of basalt, came out almost at the hollow, and halted against a side of stone. His eyes took in the men, one still on horseback, the other three dismounted. They were buffalo hunters, he confirmed, taking in the heavy .52 caliber seven-shot Spencer rifle in the saddle holster of each horse.

"Well, now, ain't this somethin' to find," he heard the one man say, a bowlegged, thick-bodied man with a heavy face. He was closest to the girls, on foot, the two others grinning just behind him. The fourth one on the horse looked on and seemed about to drool. "Shee-it," he exclaimed. "What'll the rest of the boys say when we bring these back?" He laughed, a harsh, rasping sound. He took a step forward and Karen raised her arm. Fargo saw she held a carriage whip in it.

"You stay away," she warned.

The man laughed again. "Put that little ol' thing down, sweetie, afore I shove it up your ass," he said.

"Go on, Clem, take her," one of the others said. "I'd rather have beaver than buffalo any old day." The other two guffawed.

Fargo moved forward, the Colt in his hand, positioned himself behind a little ledge of the basalt formation. The bowlegged one took another step and Karen lashed out with the whip. It caught the man across the shoulder and the side of his face. He shook it off as he would a fly, caught hold of the whip, and yanked. Karen flew forward before she could let go of the handle and he caught her by the hair, pressed her face down on the ground.

"You let her go," Fargo heard Chrissie cry out, saw her start forward, Joannie and Pam going with her, Terry and two of the others starting to join in. The two other buffalo hunters on foot sprang forward with a whoop.

"Let's fight some, yeooooweee," the one shouted, made a darting grab for Chrissie, but the girl was faster, spun away from. She backed off, the others going with her. "Come on now, sweeties, come on," the man called, his arms hanging loosely, apelike. "You three come get me. I'm waitin' here for you."

The bowlegged one holding Karen by the hair raised his arm, flipped her on her side, and Fargo heard her cry of pain as she hit the dirt. He let go of her, laughed again. It was the moment Fargo had waited for, the others back out of the line of fire. He let one shot go, creased the man's scalp as it blew his hat off. "Don't move," Fargo said as the man started to whirl for his gun. "Don't anybody move."

The men turned slowly, focusing on where the shot had come from, and Fargo's voice was quiet steel. "Get off the horse," he said. The man didn't move. Fargo fired again and the bullet blew the man's belt buckle away. Fargo watched as the rider fell from the horse in his haste to get down. "Stand over with the others," he ordered as the man picked himself up. "Now the rest of you drop your gun belts," Fargo said. "Nice and slow." They obeyed, truculence in each face, and Fargo rose to his feet, moved into sight.

"Who the hell are you?" the bowlegged one growled.

"I'm the head honcho around here, that's who," Fargo said. "This is my string and no buffalo-smelling cayuse is going to touch them."

The man frowned, his eyes darting to the girls and back to Fargo. "All of 'em yours?" he queried.

"You heard me," Fargo said. "You've got friends. Where are they?"

"Out on the prairie somewhere," the man said.

"How far out?" Fargo questioned.

"How the hell should I know? They've been riding," he growled.

"How many?" Fargo asked.

The man shrugged and Fargo saw the craftiness slip into his face. "Three more," he said.

Fargo took a step forward, pushed the Colt into the man's forehead. "You've got one more chance to tell the truth," he growled, drew the hammer back on the Colt.

"Twenty," the man said at once.

Fargo stepped back, took the gun away from the man's forehead. "They won't need you four, then, will they?" he said, leveled the Colt at the man, drew the hammer back.

"Fargo, no," Karen's voice called out. "You can't just kill them in cold blood."

"Sure I can. I'll make believe they're buffalo," Fargo said, his eyes blue agate.

"Look, mister, we didn't hurt them," the man said, the fear in his voice. "We was just going to have us some fun."

"Bullshit," Fargo barked. "The young ladies are easily upset, which makes you very lucky. Leave the horses and the guns and start walking."

"Hell, mister, give us our horses," one of the others protested. Fargo moved the Colt an inch, speared the man with his eyes.

"In two seconds I'm going to not give a damn how upset the young ladies get," he said. He saw the man swallow, turn, start to walk. The bowlegged one followed, then the other two. Fargo stepped after them as they went down the pathway, halted where he could see them as they reached the flatland. The bowlegged one glanced back, saw him watching, hurried on. Fargo waited till they were little figures dotting the vast prairie, turned, and went back to the wagons.

"Would you have killed them, Fargo?" Chrissie was the first to ask.

"I'm not much for murder," he said. "But I should have. I'll most likely have to do it anyway."

"Why?" Terry asked. "You think they'll come back?"

"I goddamn well know they'll be back, along with all of their friends," Fargo said. "That's why I sent them walking. It'll take them a day to meet up with the others, a day we can use."

"Maybe they won't bother coming back then," Karen said.

Fargo's grunt was a harsh sound. "You heard them. They'll take beaver over buffalo any day."

"How'd you know he was lying about there being only three others?" Joannie asked.

"From the tracks I saw a few days back, and buffalo hunters don't operate in seven-man packs," Fargo said, and his lips drew back in a grimace. "There'll be twenty-four of them," he murmured. "And all we have is their four rifles and my Colt. We better make time and do some fancy hiding."

"We've eight rifles," Karen said.

Fargo's brow lifted. "You've eight rifles?" he echoed.

"At the bottom of one of the wagons, in a box. I purchased them as a precaution," she said. "From a man selling them. I think he said they were called Patersons."

"Army issue," Fargo said. "Can any of you shoot?"

Six hands went up. "None of us are exactly sharp-shooters," Joannie said.

"But the rest of us can pull a trigger and we might just hit something."

Fargo's brow furrowed as he thought aloud. "The four

Spencers and eight Patersons, twelve in all, handled by amateurs, against twenty-four buffalo hunters. "Not very good odds, no matter how you slice it," he said. "That's the first thing I've got to do."

"What is the first thing?" Terry asked.

"Find a way to do something about the odds," he answered. "Get in the wagons. I'll do my thinking while we put some more distance between us. Take their four horses along."

He followed close to the hills, set a fast pace until halting to rest at midday. Katherine, Chrissie, Terry, and Pam gathered around him as he rested against a stone. He saw Karen sitting alone beside the bay, her profile etched against the sun, a delicate yet strong line.

"Miss Fisher's not talking to us. Not much, anyway," Chrissie said.

"She's still burning, I'm sure," Fargo said.

"It's more than that. She forbid us to carry on with you anymore, using her words," Chrissie said.

"But we refused to promise that," Terry said.

"That didn't go over big," Fargo remarked.

"We said we'd obey her again when we reached Beulah but not out here," Katherine added. "Everyone else backed us up."

"She didn't just take that, did she?" Fargo asked.

"Not exactly. She said anyone who carried on with you would be expelled, not allowed in the new school and sent home as soon as possible," Chrissie told him.

"Think she can make that stick?" Fargo asked.

"Sure. She can send us packing when she gets in the new school. We're in her charge," Terry said.

Fargo studied their faces, saw the threat was one they didn't relish. "Sort of a Chinese standoff, then, I'd say," he commented.

"Not to those of us who haven't had a chance yet," Pam snapped. "Miss Fisher can go to hell."

Fargo shot a glance at the girl, saw that her eyes didn't echo the angry defiance of her words. "Let's move," he said gruffly, and rose to his feet, climbed onto the pinto, and headed the wagons northwest along the edge of the hills.

It was later in the day when Karen rode up alongside him, kept her eyes straight ahead as she spoke, ice hanging on each word.

"I presume the girls told you how they defied me," she bit out. "I hope you're proud of yourself."

"You're long on orders and short on understanding," he told her. And then, a grimness moving into his voice, "It won't mean shit, none of it, unless I can figure a way to cut the odds facing us," he growled.

Her face went tight and she rode on in silence.

By midafternoon he swung the wagons back into the low hills, halted, and let them gather around the pinto. A plan had formed in his mind after he'd discarded one thought after the other, a plan that would hinge on luck and timing, but it was the only one with a ghost of a chance to work.

"We've got to make them split up," he told the others. "Maybe we'll have a chance taking on half at a time but that's the only chance we'll have."

"How do we make them split up?" Karen questioned.

"They'll pick up the wagon tracks easy as pie, but I don't figure they'll be catching up to us till sometime tomorrow and maybe not till the day after if the main group are cutting down a herd," Fargo said. "They know they can catch up to us in their own time. But when they get here, we'll give them two wagon tracks to follow."

"You're thinking that half will follow the one set and half the other," Karen put in.

"I'd make a bet on that much," he said. "Four of you will take one wagon as high into the hills here as you can and find a place to hide it. You'll walk back down here

92

and rejoin the others. In the morning, you all take the other wagon with the guns in it, and the extra horses, and move out on the plains. You go along the edge of the hills just as we've been doing."

"Where will you be?" Chrissie asked.

"I'm riding on now to find a good place to make a stand with the other wagon. I'll watch for you, come morning, and move down to meet you."

"What if the first half find the wagon we hid?" Terry asked.

"No matter," Fargo said. "I'd expect they'd stake it out and wait for somebody to come back for it, which is just what I'd like them to do." He drew a deep breath, ran his eyes over the group. "You have everything straight now?" he asked.

"Hide the one wagon, move out with the other in the morning," Karen said. "Keep going until you meet us. It's hardly very complicated."

Fargo nodded, let his eyes touch each of the girls for an instant, pause at each serious, determined young face. Shit, he swore silently as he turned and rode away.

# 6

Fargo stayed in the hills, moving as fast as the terrain would allow. When night came, he slowed but kept going, aided by a half-moon. He finally halted, slept till daybreak, and continued on. The hills had turned greener, stands of pale-barked cottonwoods with lots of shadbush. He finally halted just below a ridge, a good spot with natural cover and enough passageway up from the flatlands for the wagon. He was just about to turn and move down farther to wait for the wagon when his nose twitched, the faint smell of smoke. He sniffed again. It was wafting over the top of the ridge from the other side and he urged the pinto upward, dismounted when he neared the ridgeline, and went the rest of the way on foot.

He dropped low at the crest of the ridge, the smoke stronger, and peered down the other side of the sloping ground. The smoke spiraled lazily up from an Indian camp of four tepees. His eyes narrowed as he watched the figures below, one old man, the rest squaws and naked children. His eyes paused at the design on one tepee. Sioux, he grunted, the men off hunting someplace. The women were smoking deer meat on a high drying rack, the young girls pounding berries for use in pemmican. It was a small family camp, no war-party camp, and he turned from the top of the ridge, made his way back down to the pinto. He continued down the hills toward the prairie below, found a small ledge, and dismounted to

94

wait. It was almost noon when he spied the Conestoga rolling along the flatland, six riders alongside it. Chrissie's blond hair caught the sun as she sat one of the horses. They were moving quickly and he rode down to intercept them, came out a few dozen yards ahead of the wagon.

Joannie held the reins, Laurie beside her, and he saw Karen at the head of the riders. She came up to him quickly, her face tense. "We saw a dust spiral when we left the hills," she told him. "Way back on the horizon, but it was definitely there."

Fargo's lips pursed in thought. "Could be them if they'd been riding hard. Or could be a herd of antelope. We'll know by morning," he said. He pointed to the passageway into the hills. "Start moving the wagon up there," he called to Joannie, rode to a low-hanging length of shadbush, and broke it off. As the wagon started up the passageway, the footing underneath ridged rock, Fargo dismounted and began to sweep the trail away with the branch, using long, flat strokes. When he finished, the wagon trail into the hills had vanished. He walked back along the rest of the wagon tracks for almost a quarter-mile, sweeping them clean with the branch, then returned along the rocks at the edge of the hills. Karen, on the bay, was waiting.

"They'll see the wagon tracks just come to a halt and know you've headed into the hills," he said to the question in her eye. "But this way they won't know just where you turned off. It'll give us at least three or so more hours, maybe half a day."

He headed up the passageway, Karen following, caught up to the wagon as the horses strained to pull up a sharp incline, digging their hooves into the hard soil of the hill. "Some of you get out and walk," Fargo ordered, and the trim, lithe figures bounded from the wagon. He led them on until he reached the bottom of the last ridge, halted, and swung from the pinto.

95

"What's the plan now?" Karen said, dismounting.

"We wait until they find the wagon. They'll see enough of you with it to think we're all there. When they come down, some of us will be waiting on the higher ground and we'll nail them in a cross fire," he said, finished the rest to himself. Accurate shooting was out of the question and so the barrage of cross fire was the only hope. With a large helping of luck, it'd work. "Let's break out the rest of the rifles. We need to do some preparing and I want you to get the feel of the guns."

"Everyone get their bags and things out of the wagon," Karen ordered. "The rifles are at the bottom in a long wooden box." As the girls began unloading bags and baggage, small wooden chests and assorted boxes, Fargo went over to the pinto, loosened the girth, and checked the horse's hooves. He had just finished the last hoof when he heard the sounds from the wagon, voices raised, anger and sharp tones suddenly erupting. He peered across at the wagon. "What's the matter?" he called.

Karen's head appeared from around the end of the lowered tailgate. Her face, set tight, peered at him. "We brought the wrong wagon," she said stiffly.

Fargo stared at her. "What'd you say? I think I heard wrong," he said slowly.

Her lips pressed together. "We brought the wrong wagon. The rifles are in the other one," she said.

Fargo walked toward her in long, slow strides and he felt his hands clenching. She moved out to meet him, her eyes carrying fear but her chin high. He saw the others gathering to one side. He halted in front of her.

"Say it." She swallowed. "I know what you're thinking."

"I'm thinking of a lot of words for you and I haven't come up with the right one yet," Fargo growled.

"I thought I had the right wagon," she said, and looked

helpless. "I guess I just shuffled them around. I should have checked, I suppose."

"You should have stayed home," Fargo snapped.

"I'm sorry," she murmured, shrugged disconsolately.

"Not as sorry as you're going to be when they get hold of you," he said.

Chrissie's voice cut in. "Can't we do anything? Can't we hide or something?"

"Not for long. Without those other rifles, we've no damn chance to fight them off," Fargo said angrily.

"We'll have to go back for the other rifles," Terry cut in.

"How are you going back without their seeing you?" Fargo asked harshly.

She half-shrugged. "At night? Sneak back?"

"Can you find the other wagon at night?"

He saw her lips press onto each other, look at the others. "No, never," she murmured. "We'd have a job finding it in the daylight."

"Then that takes care of that idea," Fargo said bitterly.

"What'll we do?" Karen asked. "Nothing?"

"That might be as good an idea as any. Sit down and be quiet while I think some more," Fargo answered, walked away, and went halfway up the ridge. He sat down, his lips drawn in grimly, cursed quietly for a few minutes, then began to rack his brain for a way out. He frowned in thought for over an hour, but each idea closed off like a box canyon. When he finally rose and returned down to where the wagon waited, he had only one slender hope in hand and even that hung on the end of a large question mark.

"There's no way you'll get back to find the other wagon without being seen and caught," he told the waiting, anxious faces. "But there's one chance that might work. If I can circle around high in the hills, come down, and find the wagon before they've got to it, I can come back with the rifles. To do it you've got to describe the place where you hid it."

He waited, saw Chrissie exchange glances with Terry, the others look at one another and at Karen. He saw her shrug helplessly. "I can't describe it. We'd have to be there, see things for ourselves again, find our way," she said.

"There was a big rock next to two smaller rocks," Pam said.

"There are only about a half-million like that in these hills," Fargo returned.

"And there was a passage with a fork in it coming up from the flatland," Katherine added. "But we wouldn't know how to tell you to find it coming down from higher in the hills."

Fargo turned away, stared into space. The thin thread had torn. Circling back on his own and finding the wagon would be a matter of sheer luck and they hadn't the time for that kind of luck. His eyes went to the horses strung out behind the wagon, seven in all. With some carrying two riders they could leave everything and try to make a run for it. He shook his head. It'd give them another day or two but no more. The horses wouldn't be able to keep a hard pace carrying two riders. Getting the rifles in the other wagon was still their only chance of surviving.

"I smell smoke," Karen said, interrupting his grim thoughts.

"From the other side of the ridge," he muttered as his eyes went to the ridgeline, stayed there. The thought took a moment to be born, came in little pieces, pulling itself together slowly to finally become a whole. His frown stayed as he turned to Karen and the others. "You have jewelry, combs, pocket mirrors, stuff like that, don't you?" he asked.

"Some," Karen answered.

"Get it out—beads, necklaces, brushes, kerchiefs,

whatever you have that sparkles," he said. "Pile it on the ground here. *Now*," he barked.

There was an instant flurry of activity and the girls began digging into bags and boxes. A small mound of necklaces, assorted pins, rings, and mirrors quickly rose.

"Save some combs and brushes for yourselves," he said.

"I've an extra pair of slippers," Laurie said.

"Put 'em with the rest of the things," he told her. "And give me an old shirt."

Pam came up with a tattered blouse and he placed all the jewelry, combs, and other assorted pieces into the blouse, wrapped it up, and swung onto the pinto.

"What's all this about?" Karen asked.

"I'll tell you when I get back. You stay here and put all your things back in the wagon," he ordered, wheeled the pinto around, and started up the ridge to the crest. He slowed when he reached the top, started down the other side, moving the pinto at a very slow walk, staying out in the open, where his approach could be easily seen. As he neared the bottom of the hill and the Indian camp, he saw the squaws gather, watch apprehensively as he moved closer. An old man appeared holding a bow, arrow strung. Fargo kept the slow, steady walk as he reached the outer perimeter of the small camp. The smoke wafting over the drying racks was now a sharp, pungent odor. He halted at the edge of the camp, held up one hand in the traditional sign of peace, and spoke out in the Siouan he knew, using a mixture of Dakota and Mandan dialect.

One squaw, a parchment face on a square body, responded in Dakota Sioux, beckoned him forward. He moved slowly, saw the younger squaws gathering around, the children staying on the fringe, wide-eyed naked little bodies. The young squaws wore elkskin skirts and nothing else. He dismounted, the blouse under his arm, knelt down, and rolled it out on the ground, scattering the jewelry, combs, pocket mirrors, and all the other items across it. It was the accepted gesture of trading and the squaws came to stand in a semicircle at once, the younger ones pushing forward. They reached out, some kneeling, picked up the objects, babbled excitedly with one another. One, a tall young woman with long, swaying breasts, draped one of the necklaces around her. Fargo reached out and firmly but gently took it from her, placed it back atop the blouse.

"Trade," he said in Sioux.

The old squaw nodded, gestured for him to indicate his demands. He had already swept the camp with his eyes as they had pawed over the items he'd brought. They had what he wanted, he saw by the decorated baskets and the colors edging their tepees. Moreover, he had a good bargaining position. The jewelry and other items had them eager for trading and he'd be asking for items that were commonplace to them. He pointed to the color red on the bottom edge of a tepee design, used his knowledge of sign language to indicate the rest. The old squaw muttered to one of the younger girls who left the circle, returned a few minutes later with a small wooden bowl of red clay mixed with fish oil to make a dye. "More," he said, indicating a lot more. The girl came back with a large skin filled with the red ocher dye. Fargo took it, set it beside himself, and offered the squaw two necklaces. She insisted on a ring with it and he conceded.

He pointed to the black of the tepee decoration and once again the old squaw spoke to the girl, who reappeared carrying a large bowl of crushed elderberry mixed with a thin paste of tubers of the sumac root. Fargo passed on another three items and the squaw took them in, letting two of the younger girls take one each. He put his finger on one of the elkskin skirts. He counted ten on his fingers. The squaw nodded but demanded over half of the remaining items. He allowed himself to pause, seem to ponder the bargain, then gave in. He saved the slippers, shawls, kerchiefs, and leather gloves, along with the pocket mirrors, for last.

The old squaw was fascinated by the mirrors, he saw; she kept looking into them and frowning, unsure she was seeing herself. The others gestured, laughed, assured her the image was her own. She looked at Fargo, waited for his demand. He pointed to two old travois and a somewhat tattered scalp shirt hanging from a post of the nearest tepee. The old squaw considered for a moment, but she was not matching his performance, he knew. She was weighing the bargain to be struck with all seriousness. He decided to push and he swept his arm across the remaining material on the blouse, then reached out and took back one of the necklaces. He made another sweeping gesture and his message was plain. She'd agree to this last exchange or he'd take back everything and go on. The old squaw nodded, barked an order, and the others instantly fell upon the last items, snatching them up, the old blouse with it.

Three young boys brought the travois to him and another squaw the tattered scalp shirt. He mounted the pinto, after making a bundle of the dyes and the elk skirts and putting them on one of the travois. He rested the scalp shirt over the saddle horn and held the second travois in front of him. Pulling the other travois along flat with his lariat, he began slowly to climb back up the hill to the top of the ridge. The squaws watched him for a while, then turned their attention to the new trinkets they had traded. Fargo, moving carefully not to upset the dyes, crested the ridge and went down the other side, finally returning to the Conestoga. Everyone was standing, watching as he rode up.

"We're going to do some playacting," he said as he swung from the pinto. He saw Karen's frown as she peered at him. "We're going to move right across the flatland, under the eyes of those buffalo hunters. But what they'll see is a brave leading his squaws and a few horses across country." He carefully lifted the dyes from the travois, untied the wrappings, then tossed the elkskin skirts on the ground. "They'll have riders out searching, but they won't bother even a single brave with his squaws. That'd be looking for the kind of trouble they don't want. We'll move on to the area where you hid the wagon and then move into the hills. You'll all become squaws."

Terry picked up one of the elkskin skirts. "Just by wearing these?" She frowned.

"Hell, no. First you'll use the red ocher to color your bodies. You can do each other. Then you'll use the elderberry dye to make your hair black. All except Katherine and Chrissie. It'll look even more real if there are two white women captives. But first, some of you take that wagon deeper into the hills and hide it someplace the way you did the other. Leave the extra horses here."

Chrissie, Katherine, Laurie, Pam, and Millie Harris went off with the wagon and Fargo met Karen's eyes.

"Do you really think you can pull off this masquerade?" she questioned.

"Yes, if we do it right. It's our only chance of getting to the wagon with the rifles," he said, turned from her, and began mixing the red ocher dye, using some water from his canteen to thin the mixture. It was almost an hour when Chrissie and the others came back down and he'd just finished readying both the red ocher and the black dye of the elderberry and sumac tubers.

"We found a rock cave, put it inside, and covered the front with branches," Chrissie said.

"It'll do," Fargo said. "Now start putting the red ocher all over yourselves. Not too heavy, just a light cover will do."

He heard Karen's voice cut in, saw her holding up one

of the elkskin skirts. "There are no tops to these," she said.

"That's right," Fargo said, and saw her eyes flick to where the girls were starting to pull off blouses.

"Stop that," she called out. "What are you doing?"

"We're going to apply the dye the way Fargo wants," Terry said as she let her lovely deep breasts wriggle out of her shirt.

"This is quite unnecessary," Karen said, her eyes returning to the big, black-haired man. "You could have brought back complete deerskin dresses. You're enjoying this exhibition."

"I didn't see thirteen deerskin dresses, but they did have the skirts," he said.

"I won't be a part of walking about three-quarters naked," she said.

"This is our one chance of getting to the wagon with the rifles. You're not going to louse it up," he told her.

"I'm not parading around for your amusement. You go back and bring me a deerskin dress," she snapped.

Fargo half-turned to see the girls busily applying the dye to their bodies and to one another, turning their skins into a reddish tone. He turned back to Karen, who continued to flash fire at him. He half-smiled at her, moved casually a step closer. His hand shot out as fast as a rattlesnake's strike, clapped around her mouth, and his other arm scooped her up as though she were a rag doll. He strode off with her under his arm, went around to the other side of a boulder, and flung her to the ground. She tried to claw at him, but he turned her on her stomach, held her face into the dirt.

"Now, I'm only going to say this once, so you better hear it right. I'm not going back to get you any damn deerskin dress. All this risk is because you brought the wrong goddamn wagon and now you're going to go along

**103**

with everyone else or I'll turn your hide red another way."

He took his hand, yanked at the shirt, and tore it in two down the back and heard her muffled cry of protest. Flipping her over with one quick, harsh motion, he ripped away the rest of the shirt and watched her breasts push out, beautifully shaped with flat, light-pink tips and light-pink circles to match.

"Bastard," she hissed, tried to hit him, but he slapped her hand away and she gasped in pain. With one more quick motion, he yanked her skirt away, tearing it almost in two, pulled it free of her legs as she tried to kick him. She started to get up, clad only in white panties with lace edging, but he moved with catlike quickness, pulled her to the ground again, took a moment to enjoy the lovely long legs, well-turned calves, and nice, slender yet full thighs.

"Nice," he commented. "Damn waste, though."

"Let me go, you big bastard," she hissed at him, tried to pull away, gave up in futility to glare at him.

"Now you've only one decision to make, honey," Fargo said. "Do you put the red ocher on yourself or do I do it for you?"

Her eyes held fury, but he saw the sullen defeat creep into them. "I'll do it myself," she breathed, and he let go of her, stepped back, watched her pull herself to her feet. She did have a damn fine figure, he noted again, and she half-turned from him, covering her breasts with her hands. He reached out, yanked her hands down.

"Dammit, you're supposed to be an Indian squaw and you act like one or I'll treat you like one," he barked. "Now get the hell back with the girls and start making yourself up." She walked from him, head high, back straight, and her hands down at her sides. He followed slowly, his eyes taking in the scene. Many of the girls had finished coloring their torsos and were starting on their legs. Some were in panties, others had put on the elkskin

104

skirts. He saw Karen go off by herself with a handful of the red ocher dye and begin to rub her arms and shoulders with it. His eyes moved across the others, figures he had come to know intimately and those few he was seeing for the first time. His eyes moved back to Karen. Lovely as most of them were, there was a subtle difference in Karen's body, the additional years of maturity pulling all the young coltishness together, her movements with an added coordinated grace. Damn waste, he echoed again silently.

Joannie, Pam, and Barbara had finished and presented themselves proudly for him to admire, young breasts upturned, Frances joining them with her pillowy bosom. "Good," Fargo said, surveying the job they'd done. "I've thinned out the black hair dye. You'll not be needing it for weeks. Start giving yourself black squaw hair."

While they began to dip into the black dye, he took his straight razor from his saddlebag kit and began to shave his beard away. When he finished, he put his hat into the saddlebag and slipped on the scalp shirt. He stripped trousers off, improvised a breechcloth, and dyed his legs. It took another hour for everyone else to finish, but finally they were all red-skinned and black-haired except for Katherine and Chrissie, who stayed dressed and without disguise. Fargo took the four Spencer rifles and strapped them onto the travois, covering them with strips of cloth, adding some of the girls' shirts and riding britches knotted together to the pack, covered them with more cloth. He took the saddle from the pinto, shoved it deep under a thick stand of scrub brush, and swung onto the horse. He faced the girls, let his eyes rove across them in a last check. Karen stayed to one side by herself, her breasts turned away from him.

"Joannie and Pam, you take one travois, Barbara and Millie take the other," he said. "Chrissie and Katherine, you go along in the center of the group." He turned the pinto, sitting very straight on the horse, beckoned to Karen. She came, her eyes glowering, arms at her sides, and looking very beautiful in the short elkskin skirt. "You walk right behind me. That makes you number-one squaw," he told her.

"You'll pardon me if I'm not too honored," she bit out.

"You should be," he said, moved the pinto forward, waved a hand for the others to follow. He started down through the hills, emerged on the flatland, headed directly out onto the prairie, then turned south. He walked the pinto slowly, glanced back at the squaws marching behind him, let his eyes go down to Karen just behind the pinto. She glowed at him, lovely, firm breasts pushing out, nipples darkened by the dye now. He turned to stare ahead and sat the pinto with his back very straight, sitting the horse imperiously, Indian fashion. Riding bareback, the heat of the horse warmed his legs, no saddle in the way, rider and horse directly connected. It felt good, the one-quarter Cherokee in him coming to the fore. They had walked a few miles when, out of the corner of his eye, he picked up the line of riders to his left, just in front of the hills. He continued on, but he could feel the eyes watching them from across the prairie. He decided to embellish the role a little more for the watchers and turned the pinto to move back along the line of squaws. Frances and Susan were the last and he wheeled the horse alongside Susan, reached down, and sent her half-falling forward with a hard push. She caught herself, looked up at him, but the astonishment in her eyes turned to understanding as, from his stern face, he winked at her.

He rode up to the head of the marchers again, swung in front of Karen, and continued on. The distant line of riders began to move away as he continued the march south, refusing the trap of false security. They could have left spotters behind in the hills. It was almost a certainty, in fact. When the sun began to move toward the horizon, he turned and began to move toward the hills. He drew back to where Chrissie and Katherine trudged along. They and Terry had hidden the wagon, he remembered.

"This is about where I left you to hide the wagon. Start keeping your eyes open for anything that looks familiar," he told them. They nodded and he returned to head the march, saw that tiredness had set into Karen's face, but her mouth stayed stubbornly angry. He spoke to her without turning around. "Staying mad takes up a lot of energy," he remarked.

"That's fine with me," she snapped.

He kept riding, led the way into the hills, and halted at a rocky hillock with a trickle of water coursing down one side of the rocks. He swung down from the pinto in the gathering dusk.

"See anything?" he murmured to Terry.

She nodded. "That passage to the left. I'm sure it's the one we took up."

He grunted, watched the other girls pull the travois to the side. Karen, tired lines in her face, nonetheless kept the stubborn set of her chin and her back to him. He had chosen the place because of the water and the wild plants he had spotted. The nearest was the growth of thick plants with the long, slightly heart-shaped leaves and the tiny greenish flowers. The fleshy leafstalks wrapped themselves close to the stout stems in profuse growth. His eyes went to the yellow sunflowers on the thin stalks at the opposite side and he sat down on the ground. "Joannie, you and some of the other girls start gathering the green leaves of those plants over there. They're called dock. The rest of you dig up the tubers at the bottom of those sunflowers. You'll see them just under the ground, long and bumpy, Jerusalem artichokes."

"What are you going to do?" Karen snapped, turning.

"Sit here," Fargo said, keeping his head bent low.

"Aren't you carrying this a little far?" she shot back.

107

"No, Miss Fisher Bigmouth," he growled. "They're probably keeping an eye on us while they're looking around. We make one false move and they'll be down on us like buzzards on a carcass. A Sioux brave wouldn't be gathering up dinner with all his squaws around. Now move your damn ass and start picking those tubers."

He didn't raise his head but saw her get to her feet out of the corner of his eye, march to where the tall sunflowers grew against the rocks. He had Chrissie make a fire as the night descended. "I put an iron pot from one of the wagons onto the travois," he told her. "Fill it with water and set it on the fire till it boils, then put the leaves of the dock in it. When the leaves are almost done, put in the tubers and simmer them about fifteen minutes."

He sat back and watched as the leaves were picked from the dock, torn in halves, and dropped into the boiling water. "Spread them out on a rock and eat with your fingers," he said when they were done. While the Jerusalem artichokes simmered, the girls gathered around and ate the boiled dock, savoring the slightly bitter, lemonish flavor. "Some folks call it wild spinach," he told them. He used his knife to peel and slice the Jerusalem artichokes when they were ready and slowly munched on the potatolike tubers given added taste by the dock-flavored water.

Karen sat at the very edge of the firelight, letting the dark clothe her nakedness as much as she could, and he spoke to Terry without looking at her. "See anything that looks familiar?" he asked.

She nodded. "The passage, it goes up past a row of little stones. I'm sure it's the one we used."

"We'll find out later," he answered. He stretched out, arms behind his head. "Curl up by yourselves and let the fire go out," he said. He lay half-awake, watched the flickering light go out and blackness take over the hollow. A half-moon rose to restore a dim light. He waited an hour more, then rose to his feet, silent as a mountain lion on the prowl. He tapped Terry and Chrissie and the girls sat up. He motioned for silence with a finger against his lips and they rose, started to go with him. "Which way?" he whispered.

Terry gestured to the passage and he followed. She and Chrissie climbed upward to halt at a place where the passageway became two. They peered at the rocks and Chrissie gestured to a gnarled, windblown shadbush. Terry nodded and they moved upward again along the path to the left. Fargo followed until they halted again at another turnoff. They murmured, frowned, were plainly uncertain.

"Take your time. Think back," he said.

"That rock with the split along one edge, I remember it," Terry said. "Don't you? We went left again here."

Chrissie frowned. "Maybe," she agreed. "I kind of remember it."

They started off and he was on their heels as they followed a pathway hardly wide enough to accommodate the Conestoga. They climbed higher and he was beginning to wonder if Terry hadn't made a mistake when they emerged onto a flat alcove. Terry pointed to a cluster of hop hornbeam and he saw Chrissie agree with an excited nod. He went with them as they dashed for the thick tree cover and he saw the wide space between two of the trees, extra branches stuck up onto the trees to close off the space. He climbed through with them to see the Conestoga hidden amid the trees, and he smiled for the first time all day. With the girls' help, he dug through traveling bags to reach the long, flat wooden box, pulled it out, and yanked the top from it. The eight Army-issue Paterson rifles met his eyes, glinting faintly in the moonlight.

He scooped out four, handed them to Terry, took the other four himself, and had Chrissie carry the two boxes of ammunition.

"What now?" Terry asked as they started downward.

"We move out right away, get back to where we left the other wagon before they find it," he said. "I think we can make it back before daybreak, but in any case we go the way we came, a brave and his squaws, just in case we run into any of them."

"And after we get to the wagon?"

"We'll set up a mousetrap as best we can," he told her. He led the way back down; the others were awake or woke at once when they arrived. Fargo cautioned for silence again, put the rifles on the travois, and covered them. He climbed onto the pinto, pressed his heels gently into the horse's ribs, and started the rest of the way down to the flatland. He refused to hurry, maintaining the same slow pace as they headed back through the night, the half-moon affording enough light to keep the path parallel to the hills. He glanced back, his eyes pausing on Karen just behind him, then sweeping the rest of his bare-busted troupe. A wave of excited confidence had run through them when he'd returned with the rifles and he'd let it stay, but he knew it was more than a little hasty. Getting the rifles back was the first step, but only that. If he couldn't set up a trap, and if they couldn't close it hard, it'd all mean nothing. His mind turned to the job ahead as he led the way and suddenly felt a little like Moses leading the children through the wilderness, only he didn't have the friend in high places old man Moses had.

# 7

He was glad to see the first hesitant light of day and his eyes swept the line of the hills at once. They had overshot the spot where they'd come down to the plains by a hundred yards or so and he led the way back as they moved toward the hills. His glance swept the horizon and then scanned the land behind them; he saw nothing. But before the morning was old their pursuers would have two bands riding, one moving along the prairie, the other searching the hills.

Fargo led the way onto the pathway leading upward, climbed until they'd gone halfway up. He halted and swung from the pinto. "Go get the wagon and bring it down here," he told Laurie and Pam. "Use two of the horses." He untied the half-hitches in the tethers as the girls climbed onto the horses and galloped off. He turned to the others at once. Every second was important now and Joannie voiced the question in all their waiting eyes.

"What next?" she asked.

"The squaws disappear. You've got to go back to being yourselves. When the wagon gets here, use the water in the kegs to wash the dye out of your hair, then rinse your faces clean. Get into your clothes as soon as you're dry," he said. "While you're waiting, get the rifles off the travois and load them."

As the girls rushed to follow his orders, he found the thick scrub brush where he'd hidden the saddle, pulled it out, and tightened it on the pinto. He tore off the scalp shirt, retrieved his hat, and put on his clothes, adjusting his gun belt. He turned to watch the girls handling the rifles. He gave those who had shooting experience the Spencer rifles he had taken from the buffalo hunters. They were faster and more powerful than the Army Patersons. He turned as he heard the wagon approaching, watched the big Conestoga roll down to a skidding halt. "Get the dye out of your hair," he barked, and Karen was the first at the water kegs, he noted, rinsing her hair vigorously. It took several rinsings for each girl to remove the dye and they were well into the water of the second keg by the time they had their faces rinsed. He watched Karen yank her things from the wagon, draw a shirt over herself, and glare at him as she saw his eyes on her.

"I'm surprised you haven't thought of another reason for us to stay half-naked," she said.

"I'm working on it," he said mildly, and she went around to the other side of the wagon to put on her riding britches. He turned to survey the others. They were transformed back to their former selves, perhaps even a little more shiny-faced than before, blond heads shining in the new sun, brunettes catching the rays to send off brown glints. His eyes went to the sky, saw the sun moving higher quickly. They had perhaps another hour, he guessed. "Let's move," he said. "Some of you ride the horses, the rest of you take the wagon."

He started off, led the wagon along a rocky, winding pathway through the lower hills, his eyes searching the land on both sides. He halted, finally, focusing on a thick stand of hawthorns topping a crest overlooking a small dip. He peered at the hawthorns, none of them over eight feet high, dense cover with their widespread, thorny branches. "Take the wagon down into the little dip," he ordered, followed as Pam drove the Conestoga to a halt. He dismounted and the others slid from their horses.

"Tether the extra horses over there, against that far side," he said. His glance swept the girls and he beckoned to Chrissie, Frances, Joannie, and Millie Harris.

"You four will be the bait," he said. "Make a small fire and start cooking something, anything. One of you stretch out against the rear wheel of the wagon and make like you're half-asleep. The six of you that can shoot get inside the wagon. Loosen the side flap but leave it down. You stay there and don't come out for anything." He let his eyes take in Doris and Alice, the only two left, then Karen. With himself, they'd make four to form the other half of the trap. He brought his gaze back to the six who were to go into the wagon. "You'll hear them when they arrive," he said. "But you just stay hidden inside the wagon until you hear us start firing from behind those hawthorns up there. Then you flip up the canvas and start shooting as fast as you can. If it works right, we'll cut them down pretty damn quick in the cross fire."

He peered at each grave face. "You may have to wait in there for an hour or for six hours. Whatever it is, you've got to stay hidden inside, you understand?" They nodded as one. "Any questions?" he asked.

"What do we do when they come?" Chrissie asked.

"Look scared," he told her. "You're strictly bait. I'm guessing they'll see you and the wagon and figure the others are nearby someplace." He waved an arm at Karen and the last two girls, started to climb up toward the hawthorns. He glanced back as he neared the crest, saw Terry disappearing into the wagon, the last of those who'd form the other half of the mousetrap. Frances and Millie Harris were starting to build a small fire and he continued on to the crest. Karen brushed against him as he opened a path through the thick leaves of the hawthorns, avoiding the thorny branches as best he could. He knelt down inside the cover, then stretched out, his Sharps carbine in his hand. Karen positioned herself next to him with the

113

Paterson, Doris and Laurie beside her. He could see clearly down into the little dip, the Conestoga to one side, Chrissie leaning against the rear wheel, Frances and Joannie cooking over the little fire, and Millie Harris combing her hair.

He grunted in satisfaction. It looked good. Luck had stayed with them so far and he let himself hope it would hang on just a little longer. "I've never shot a rifle before," he heard Doris whisper.

"Practice looking through the sights," he said. "When the time comes, don't bother trying to be accurate. Just fire down into them as fast as you can." He looked over Karen at the two girls. "Relax," he said. "Take your fingers off the triggers. We'll be waiting a while."

He lay the big Sharps down in front of him, stretched out, and relaxed his muscles and saw the girls follow his example.

Karen rested her gun on the grass, but the tension stayed in her and she looked at him, defensiveness in her eyes. "You still blame me for all of it, don't you?" she said.

"Who else?" he said coldly. "The whole damn trip was your baby."

She looked away but not before he'd caught the flash of hurt in her eyes. "I did what I thought was best," she murmured, not looking at him.

"Best for yourself," he said, and this time she looked at him, quick anger exploding in her eyes.

"Don't you ever ease up on anyone?" she threw back.

"Sure," he said. "When they stop making excuses to themselves." Her lips pressed hard against each other and she fell silent. Fargo turned on his back, stretched, and hoped the girls would follow his example. It wasn't likely, he realized. You learned how to wait. It took years and some people never learned. He guessed that a little over an hour had gone by when the sound caught his ears, the

114

clink of metal, a stirrup knocking against rock. He was on his stomach instantly, eyes narrowed as he peered through the leaves and branches, his gaze sweeping the rocks just above and to the left. The first rider came through a narrow crack, barely wide enough for the horse, and he moved out to his right when he was through to let the others emerge. Fargo saw him point down to the wagon, let his own gaze go down to the little hollow. Chrissie seemed asleep. Joannie and Frances, also. Millie Harris poked at the little fire and the wagon seemed harmless.

His eyes went back to the buffalo hunters and he recognized the bowlegged one on a dark-gray horse, sitting beside a white-bearded man with a harsh mouth on a red roan. They spoke in half-whispers, used their hands a lot, and Fargo saw the bowlegged one point to the wagon. It was plain that he thought most of the girls were resting inside. The cruel-mouth man raised his arm in a gesture to the right and then to the left and Fargo saw the riders began to file down toward the hollow from two sides, taking narrow passages behind rocks that would bring them into view again when they emerged at the hollow. He also saw that they had left one rider behind on the high rocks. Fargo half-smiled. The bowlegged one remembered how he had appeared to get the drop on him. The sentinel left behind was insurance against that happening again. Fargo counted the riders as they disappeared into the passages.

"Ten," he grunted. "That means the rest of them are out riding the prairie. Damn," he swore softly. "I hoped we could take all of them at once."

He pressed his lips tight. Half a loaf was better than none, and he waited, watched, and the riders came charging out of the passages and into the hollow, reined to a halt. He saw Joannie, Frances, and Millie leap up, run to where Chrissie sat by the rear wheel of the wagon, the fear in their faces all too real. He could hear the voices as they rose up from the hollow.

"Well, now, I told you we'd be back," the bowlegged one said. "Now we're going to have us that party I promised you pretty little things."

Fargo brought the Sharps up. "Fire on three," he muttered, and counted quickly. "One—two—*three!*" The other rifles exploded in a hail of gunfire, raining bullets down onto the riders. But Fargo's first shot was aimed at the top of the rocks and he saw the rider raise up in the saddle, his back arching as he seemed to catapult over the horse's rump. Fargo swung the rifle back to fire down into the hollow and he saw the wagon had erupted in a blaze of gunfire, the rifles poking out from beneath the edge of the canvas. The trap was working perfectly, the buffalo hunters toppling out of the saddles like ninepins in a bowling alley as the cross fire continued to pour into them. Fargo saw two of them bend low in the saddle and try to race out the other side of the little hollow. He followed with the rifle, fired twice, and the horses kept galloping without their riders.

"Hold your fire," Fargo called out, bellowed it again, and the rifles in the wagon sputtered into silence. "Come on, let's get down there," he muttered, and began pushing through the branches. He half-ran, half-slid down to the wagon, the hollow strewn with dead bodies. The girls had raised the canvas side of the Conestoga and he saw their faces as they stared out at the scene.

"Save going to pieces for later," he barked harshly. "You're not through yet." Karen came up beside him, frowning up at him. "The others heard the shooting. They'll be coming hell-bent-for-leather," he said.

"How soon?"

"That depends on where they are. In any case, we'll need a better place than this to make a stand. There'll be no surprise on our side this time. Get the wagon turned. Some of you take the extra horses," he ordered.

He crossed the hollow in three long strides and vaulted

into the saddle. Chrissie had climbed onto the driver's seat of the Conestoga, snapped the reins, and started to turn the wagon in a tight circle. Karen, astride the bay, started after Fargo as he motioned to the path leading down hill.

"Reload," he yelled back to the girls in the wagon as he led the way. They'd gone only a hundred yards when he heard the thunder of hooves ahead and the first of the riders came into view.

*"Goddamn!"* Fargo swore. He had hoped for at least a half-hour to find a good place. They must have been right at the edge of the hills when the shooting erupted.

He wheeled the pinto as the men glimpsed him and two shots slammed into the stone near his head at once. "Turn the wagon sideways," he yelled as he raced back, seized one of the horses by the bridle, and helped push him around. "That's it, block off the passage," he said as Chrissie swung the wagon; he leaped from the pinto, squeezed through the small space between the tail of the Conestoga and the rocks. Karen had already gone through and dismounted, and he pulled himself up into the Conestoga, checked the girls inside as three of the buffalo hunters came into view, reined up sharply. "Fire," he barked, and the rifles exploded, the noise doubly loud in the narrow passageway.

The riders ducked away, pulled their horses back, and disappeared from sight. He heard them galloping back in the passage. His eyes swept the girls, saw their faces were grave but determination wiping away shock. They'd hold together for a while longer. "If they show, you fire," he told them, and hopped down from the Conestoga. "The rest of you get under the wagon and face the other way," he ordered. "They'll be sending some to circle behind us." He stepped back as Karen led the others under the Conestoga, laid down on her stomach at the end near the front of the wagon, the rest of the girls lined up beside

**117**

her, rifles ready. Fargo took up a position at the tailgate and scanned the hills. A narrow passage between rocks opened just behind him, too narrow for them to use. They'd have to come down the main passageway from either side to mount a real attack and he had both sides covered, he mused. He shifted himself, raised the big Sharps, and let his eyes travel along the top of the rocks. They might try to pepper the wagon with gunfire from up there. It was their best bet, but to do so they'd have to come into view and that would be his job, he told himself.

He hadn't long to wait when a head appeared high atop the rocks, another following it. He fired at once, the shot short by a fraction, sending up a tiny spiral of rock fragments, and both heads ducked back out of sight. He kept the rifle trained at the top of the rocks, but no one else appeared and he finally lowered the gun, cast a quick glance at the wagon, saw Karen's eyes on him. He shifted position again, hunkered down by the tailgate for a better angle, and waited. The minutes went by, perhaps ten, then fifteen, and suddenly there was a shot, one lone shot into the air from the high ground. He saw Karen's eyes go to him again, frown.

His mind raced and his lips drew back. "Get ready," he called out, and seconds later, they came into view, racing toward the wagon from both ends of the passage. The girls fired almost as one, sending a barrage of lead in both directions. Fargo saw the riders pull up at once, wheel, race away, one trailing blood from his shoulder. He held his own fire and scanned the top of the rocks to make sure they hadn't left one behind to pour a few shots down at the same time. But the rocks remained empty and silent and he relaxed after a few moments.

"Reload," he called to the girls. "You did well. I don't think they'll try that one right soon again."

"What will they try?" Karen asked.

He shrugged. "Maybe a wild rush from one side," he

speculated. "Or maybe trying to slip closer on foot. I'll keep my eyes open for that." He leaned back against an edge of rock, his glance traveling back and forth, up and down, covering each side of the passageway and moving along the top of the rocks in a methodical pattern. But nothing moved anywhere. A half-hour passed, became almost an hour, then the four heads popped up at once, rifles firing furiously. Fargo swung the Sharps up, fired back, and the heads ducked out of sight at once. He waited for them to reappear, but they stayed out of sight as his eyes went to the wagon.

"Anybody hit?" he called.

Terry answered from inside the Conestoga. "No."

"Not under here," Karen said, and then he saw the water pouring out of the last of the full kegs. As he watched, the last trickled out and but a few drops dripped from the four holes. Fargo's eyes narrowed and he felt the uneasiness stir inside him.

"The water," he heard Barbara cry out, suddenly noticing what had happened.

"I know," he said, keeping his voice calm. "Better the keg than you." He sat back, scanned the rocks again, but nothing but sky appeared behind the topline. The sun was directly overhead and he knew the inside of the wagon was growing into a hotbox, the area below not much better. "Relax," he called softly. "They're going to wait for a while."

He made himself more comfortable against a rock, watched the time move on to an hour, then two hours and into three. Nothing moved, stirred, rustled, only the silence and the hot sun baking the pass. It was Joannie's voice that broke the silence, bursting out with the thin edge of hysterics in it. "What are they doing?" she cried.

Fargo spoke quickly, keeping his voice calm. "Trying to figure a way to get to us," he said. "They know we've got them backed off."

"I'm dying of thirst," Barbara said.

"And I'm burning up in here," Laurie put in.

"Hang in," Fargo said reassuringly. "The sun will be dropping off soon. Everything will be all right."

He watched as Karen wriggled out from beneath the wagon, leaving the rifle in place, made her way to him. "You're lying," she said, keeping her voice low. "They've got us trapped. They shot the water kegs out on purpose."

"Maybe," he allowed quietly.

"They'll just sit us out until we crack. We can't last without water," she said.

Fargo's lips pursed in thought. "They're not the kind for long sieges. They're not the Sioux. They just put some added pressure on by shooting out the water kegs. They've something else in mind."

"Such as?" she prodded.

He shrugged. "I haven't figured that out yet," he admitted. "But they'll make some move. Now get back under the wagon."

She gave him a disbelieving glance and returned to her place beneath the Conestoga, her face grim. He frowned up at the high rocks. Patience wasn't part of their makeup. You didn't need patience to hunt buffalo, unlike deer or antelope. But of course they'd riddled the water kegs on purpose. He hadn't dissuaded her about that. Damn, he swore inwardly. They were taking their own good time, whatever they had in mind. The sun had begun to sink in the distance when the voice echoed down to the pass from the rocks above.

"Ho, down there . . . let's talk some," the voice called.

Fargo rose on one knee, the rifle ready, his eyes on the high rocks, but no one came into view. "You talk. We'll listen," he called back.

"It looks like we got us a Chinese standoff here," the

120

disembodied voice said. "But soon you're going to get awful thirsty down there." The voice waited.

"Go on," Fargo said.

"Only trouble is we don't have all that much time to waste on you," the voice said. "But you done a real job on a lot of my boys and we don't aim to leave empty-handed."

"What's the deal?" Fargo cut in impatiently.

"One of those little ladies comes with us and the rest of you can go your way," the voice said.

"If it's no?" Fargo asked.

"We'll just sit here and watch you die of thirst or cut you down if you try to make a break for it," the voice said. Fargo's eyes scanned the top of the hills but no head appeared. "Just one of your pretty little things and the rest of you go free. Hell, that's a good deal," the voice said.

"That's a shit deal," Fargo said, his eyes still sweeping the rocks.

"You'll all shrivel your damn selves up down there if you don't take it, mister," the voice warned. "You can't get out."

"Go to hell," Fargo called back.

*"Miss Fisher!"* It was Terry's voice cutting through, and Fargo whirled just in time to see Karen disappearing into a cleft of rock on the other side.

"I'm coming up. We'll take the deal," he heard her call out.

"Goddamn, come back here, you little fool," Fargo called.

Karen didn't answer, but he heard her clambering up the narrow passageway. He saw the girls looking at him, shock and fear on their faces.

"Stay here," he snapped out at them. "And stay alert." He whirled, stepped into the narrow defile in the rock just back of where he'd rested. It rose sharply, came cool and

121

dark, barely wide enough for his shoulders to fit through. He half-ran, half-climbed, following the cut in the rocks as it led upward. He'd come out on the opposite side of the high rocks from where Karen would emerge and there'd be ten waiting for her. He wouldn't need to wipe out all ten, he was confident, just enough to send the rest hightailing. They were already unwilling to lose any more of their number or they'd have made a greater effort to rush the wagon.

He continued climbing, slowed as the defile ended, and he had to move out into a clear space. He knelt down, poked his head out, saw he was still a good distance from the top of the rocks. He darted across the small open space and into the safety of the next line of rocks. Holding the Sharps in one hand made climbing slow as he made his way over smooth stones that afforded little foothold, crawled on his belly across others, and finally saw the top of the rocks just ahead. He stayed down, crept the last few yards upward, and lay flat. His eyes moved across the rocks and saw the three men kneeling, waiting, clustered at the other end of the line of rock. He let his eyes move back deeper on the top ledge until he saw the others, waiting with the horses.

He brought the rifle up, rested it against a flat piece of stone, and sighted in on the trio at the other side. He counted off three imaginary shots, half-turned on his back, and drew a bead on the cluster of riders waiting back deeper. He returned to his position and waited. Karen took another few minutes to make it to the top, but he saw her appear, walking very straight as she came up out of the defile in the rocks. One of the men advanced toward her, took her by the arm; she tried to shake him off, but he hung on to her. The other two were standing together and Fargo nodded approvingly as he put his eye to the rifle sights. Karen's face was white and strained, he saw, her mouth drawn in. He passed the sights on to the

122

nearest two men, drew the Colt from his holster, and laid it on the rock beside the rifle.

He sighted once more, then fired off the first two shots. The two figures pitched foward as one, as though they were puppets suddenly pulled from their feet. The one holding Karen's arm started to bring up his rifle, trying to zero in on the marksman. He got the rifle up as far as his chest when Fargo's shot slammed into him and he spun around as though he were a top, finally sprawling facedown, his rifle falling off the edge of the rocks. Fargo had already whirled on his side, blasted two more shots into the others, not taking the time to aim. But the shots had the desired effect as the others scattered for safety. Fargo, on his feet, raced bent over across the rocks to where Karen stood frozen, unmoving. He slammed into her, taking her down with him, clinging to her as they landed on the rock. He saw a little hollow in the rock, rolled into it, pulling her with him as two shots winged just over his head.

"Damn little fool," he hissed at her as he peered over the lip of the rock.

Two shots slammed close by, but they were fired too fast. He didn't move, squinted at the small patch of brush that managed to grow out of the rock. He saw the horses first, coming into view over the top of the brush, then the riders as they charged out at full gallop. They were firing as they raced across the top of the rocks, heading for the path down at the distant end of the slope. Their shots slammed into the rock where he lay, no attempt at accuracy, just a covering fire. He ducked down, waited a second, then rose up and fired a single shot at the seven fleeing riders. The seven became six as one flew from the saddle to smash against the rocks and lay still.

They disappeared down the distant path. It'd take them down on the other side of the hills and they'd work their way back to the prairie farther on down. It was over.

123

They'd had more than enough. He turned in the little hollow of stone to look at Karen. She met his eyes with a steady answering glance. "That was the most damnfool thing I ever saw," he growled at her. "You've got a real talent for dumb things."

"It wasn't a dumb thing," she said, anger in her eyes at once. "It's been all my fault, from the very start. You said so often enough. I even brought you the wrong wagon. I couldn't just sit by and let all of those girls die."

"So you decided to get noble," Fargo grunted.

"That's rotten," she spit back. "I didn't think about being noble. I did it because I brought them to this. It was my responsibility."

"It was still damnfool dumb," Fargo told her. "You think they would have kept their word after they got hold of you?" He saw her mouth fall open, her eyes widen. "Dumb and naïve," he grunted. "They'd have had their fun with you, then used you to pressure the girls for another deal, and finally finish the others off." She stared at him, the terrible realization sinking in and her eyes round, wide saucers. He rose, reached down, and pulled her to her feet. "School's over. Let's get back down."

He led the way down the defile and heard the excited cries as he emerged with Karen in tow. The girls tumbled from the wagon, climbed out from underneath it, flinging their arms around him and around Karen.

"God, we were so afraid," Chrissie said to him. "We heard the shots and then the sound of the horses. We didn't know what had happened."

"They decided the price was getting too heavy," he said. "Get yourselves together and let's travel some while we still have daylight." He watched them clamber back into the wagon and mount the extra horses and he wheeled the pinto away, decided to say nothing about the fear that lay on him like an unseen cloak. If all the damn shooting had attracted the Sioux, it was the end of the road. He led the group down to the flatland and headed west, his eyes searching the distance for any sign of Sioux. They managed another two hours before the light faded and he camped the wagons at the edge of the hills, took his own bedroll up atop a ledge of higher ground far enough away for privacy. It was Terry who came to him, took him aside, when he returned to the camp to eat with them.

"I don't think anyone will be coming up to see you later, Fargo," she said reluctantly.

Fargo studied her face, saw something sticking just back of her troubled eyes. "It's a free country," he said gently.

"Dammit, it's not that we don't want to," the girl said, rushing words. Fargo waited. "It's Miss Fisher," she said.

"She set down another ultimatum?" Fargo asked in some surprise.

Terry continued to look uncomfortable. "No, nothing like that at all. But we were thinking about what she tried to do for us and it sort of made us see her differently. She's tried to protect us in her own way. We don't agree with her about our visiting you, but we talked about it and decided we ought to respect her wishes," Terry said. "I guess it's our way of thanking her for what she tried to do for us today." She paused, looked sharply at him. "Are we being silly about this?" she asked unhappily.

His smile was slow. Youth and ideals were showing. It was a good thing, something to let them hang on to as long as they could. He wasn't about to take it from them. "No, you're not being silly and I understand," he told her. "I'll be there if anyone changes her mind."

Terry leaned forward, kissed his cheek. "Thanks," she whispered, and he gave her rear a gentle pat as she hurried away. After eating, he returned to the high place and his bedroll. The night was warm and he stretched out in his trunks. He'd almost gone to sleep when he heard the footsteps, snapped awake instantly. The footsteps grew louder, coming up the little side path to the ledge. A wry smile touched his face. They'd had second thoughts pretty damn fast. He watched the figure come into sight and he sat up, his brows lifting.

"I haven't had a chance to talk to you alone," Karen said, and he took in the bathrobe she had wrapped tightly around her. "I want to thank you for today," she said.

"I hate wasted gestures and that would have been one," he said.

"Nevertheless, you came after me, you saved me," she said. "I can't say anything but thank you." She made a little face, threw her hands up in a gesture of annoyance. "It's such a little word, isn't it?" she commented.

"It's big enough," he said.

Her eyes stayed on him. "Yes, I suppose it is, for some people. You're a man of constant surprises."

"Yep," he agreed. "Is that the only reason you came up here, to thank me?"

"Why, yes," she said, and he saw her begin to bristle. "You certainly don't think I had any other reason, do you?"

"I do," he said quietly.

"Well, I don't. I'm not going to replace your former teenage harem. That's ridiculous," she said sniffing.

"Is it?" he asked, stepped toward her, his hand closing around the neck of her robe. He drew her to him, pressed his mouth on hers. Her lips stayed closed for a moment, softened, opened a fraction.

"Yes," she breathed. "Stop this. Stop it now."

He forced her mouth open, let his tongue move in, caressed her; her lips twitched, then opened for him, her own tongue coming forward. "No," he heard her say as her tongue darted, curled, asked. His hands slipped inside the robe, found only warm flesh, and he pushed the robe open, stepped back, swung her up into his arms and down

126

onto the bedroll. His head pressed into the firm, upturned breasts and she cried out, offered the flat light-pink circles to him. He took one, then the other, caressing, drawing them deep into his mouth. His hands moved down her body, warm wanting flesh, and he found the dark nubby brush. "Oh, Fargo . . . oh, God almighty," she gasped, and her legs began to open and close, quick, eager movements. Karen's hands drew along his back, her nails digging in, a faint tingling sensation. "Yes, yes, oh, Fargo, yes," she cried out, pulled him to her, tried to push under him with her hips. "Aaaaiiiii . . ." she cried out as his fingers caressed, explored, opened the dark and secret places. A sudden frantic desire swept through her and she pulled away from him only to virtually leap onto him, her legs coming up to dig into his hips as she tried to thrust herself onto the lancing flesh. She kept missing in her frantic haste, each time groaning in despair. He moved, rolled with her, slid deep into her, and her scream was made of wild ecstasy.

She clung to him, pushing hard, taking in all of him she could accommodate and crying out little sounds because she could hold no more. Her hands beat against his shoulders as he moved with her, slowly, then quickening the pace, letting it slow again, and she called out in protest as he pulled back and held right at the very edge. "No, no, goddamn, no," she cried in a breathy shout. He stayed poised and heard her imploring sobs, came forward with a tremendous push, and her breath caught in her throat, became a sigh from some private world of her own. The moment of moments for her seemed to explode without warning, and suddenly she was throbbing under him and he felt the softness of her contracting around him, tiny little grabbings that she made more wonderful by rolling her pelvis. "Ai . . . ai . . . aiiiiii," she screamed as the ecstasy exploded and time whirled away and her legs were soft clamps around him.

He held her, stayed with her, throbbing inside her until she slid backward to the ground, breathing harshly, and he saw her eyes staring at him, deep dark fires inside the round orbs. "Bastard," she breathed. "Bastard." He grinned down at her. She made the word into an accolade.

"Bitch," he said softly. "Wild little bitch."

She nodded. "Yes," she breathed. "Damn you, yes."

He saw the wild light come into her eyes and she was pushing up against him again, asking for more, her firm breasts lifting against his chest. She took one in her hand, pressed it into his mouth, and cried out in absolute pleasure. The moment came suddenly again when it did, the explosion of pelvic throbbing signaling the time had come, and when it ended, she lay breathing heavily in the exhaustion of passion. He watched her as she lay beside him, slowly regaining her breath, her firm lovely body a joy to behold, a body that flowed perfectly from one part to another.

She lifted herself on one elbow as her breath returned. "Were any of them more woman than that?" she asked.

"No," he admitted. His smile twinkled in the lake-blue eyes. "I wonder what they'd say if I told them Miss Fisher was taking up where they left off."

She sat up, alarm flooding her face. "You wouldn't," she said, and looked terribly beautiful with her breasts turned up proudly.

"That depends," he said.

"On what?"

"On you promising to come visit me every night," he said.

"Blackmail?"

"Giving you a reason to do what you want to do anyway," he told her.

She couldn't keep the smile back. "You really are a bastard," she murmured.

"But a right one," he said, and she nodded.

"They're all asleep by now. They're exhausted, but I'd best get back," she said, rose, and he put the robe around her. She clung to him for a moment. "You're funny-wonderful, Fargo," she said.

"And you're schoolteacher-sexpot," he said.

She chuckled quietly as she hurried away.

He lay down, drew the bedroll over himself. Self-discipline was a wonderful thing, he murmured as he went to sleep.

# 8

Except for those nights when they camped out on the prairie, Karen kept her promise and Fargo saw to it that there were only a few of those nights. He skirted the edge of the Black Hills and headed north, avoiding the most difficult passages, then moved alongside the headwaters of the Missouri. Quiet places and hidden-away nooks were plentiful there.

By day, Karen was the schoolmistress, keeping the girls in hand and balancing friendship with authority, camaraderie with discipline; by night she was a wild, wanton package shedding all surface veneer. And he enjoyed both sides of her, especially the one that was his alone. "Stay, Fargo, when we get to Beulah. I'll have a place of my own then," she told him one night.

"We'll see," he said, and they both knew better. They made good time and he showed the girls how to live off the country with wild edibles. He was letting himself feel optimistic when the time came to ford a narrow place in the Missouri and head west. "Straight for Beulah now," he told Karen as he paralleled the riverbank where the Missouri headwaters turned due west, also.

"And we're all here, Fargo. You'll be getting all of your twelve hundred dollars," she commented.

He gave a wry snort. He couldn't think about the girls in just that way any longer, he realized. He'd grown too fond of them, come to enjoy each; Chrissie with her bubbling openness, Terry and her banked fires, Katherine's direct sensuousness, Barbara's joy in finding herself, Laurie's sweet shyness, each beguiling in her own way. Their warmth and fondness for him carried beyond the times they had stolen away to visit him. He was happy that they'd come this far alive and well. Luck had been with them, he told himself.

The mellow feeling ended abruptly on a warm morning when the first light of day filtered through the trees of the small glen where they'd camped. It was Chrissie's voice he heard, a whispered call full of fear, and he woke at the sound. *"Fargo! Fargo, wake up,"* the hoarse whisper drifted to where he'd placed his bedroll. He came awake instantly, squinted through the trees. There were eight of them, sitting like stone figures on their ponies, motionless, silent, black piercing eyes fixed on the Conestoga and the sleeping figures around it. Chrissie was sitting up, eyes wide, and he saw Terry come awake, the others following, rising to stare out at the statuelike figures. Karen woke, blinked, and he saw her quick glance at him, the fear in her face.

Fargo's gaze went back to the bronzed figures, naked except for a breechcloth, two holding lances, the rest with their bows strung. The tall one in the center wore an armband and Fargo studied the beaded decorative work on it, the circle within a larger decorated circle, small designs radiating from the main circle. Mandan, he grunted silently, wandering over from Montana way, probably. He slowly drew on trousers, strapped on his gun belt. Everyone else was awake now, most on their feet, staring at the silent, unmoving figures. Fargo's eyes swept past the line of horsemen, returned when he was satisfied there were no others near by. He stepped into the half-circle made by the girls, kept his eyes on the redmen as he spoke softly through hardly moving lips.

131

"I'm going to challenge the one with the armband," he muttered. "Try to put it on a man-to-man basis."

"Will that work?" Karen whispered back.

"Probably not. He's got no reason to go for it," Fargo said. "But it'll buy us a little time. The rifles are in the wagon. I want you to file in through the tailgate, each take a rifle, and come out the front with the rifle under your robes or dresses. They won't be expecting gunfire from you."

"When do we shoot?" Karen asked.

"When they go for me. And you'd better shoot quick or you'll need a new trailsman," he said.

He waited for a moment as the girls began to file into the Conestoga, Chrissie first, Barbara behind her, then Karen, the others lining up. The Indians still remained motionless and Fargo moved toward them, walking with slow, deliberate steps. He saw their eyes swing to him and he focused on the one with the armband. The Mandan spoke a Sioux dialect. They'd understand him. He halted a few yards from the row of horses, kept his eyes on the tall one with the armband and the lance in his hand. He gestured to the girls filing into the wagon and then to himself.

"Mine," he said. "You can take horses."

The Indian shook his head, a barely perceptible movement.

"Mine," Fargo repeated, cast a glance back at the wagon. The girls were filing out of the other end now, walking stiffly, turning to face the Indians. Fargo looked at the tall one again and made the Sioux sign for combat, touched his chest, and pointed at the brave. The Indian's black eyes stared impassively at him. Fargo repeated the gesture and the Indian remained motionless.

"Squaw," Fargo flung out. "Afraid."

He saw the Indian's eyes flicker for just an instant, return to impassiveness. Fargo spit on the ground and watched the man's hand holding the lance. He saw the fingers tighten, the wrist begin to flex. He was diving to one side as the yell exploded, the motionless figure erupting into action. Fargo hit the ground as the lance grazed his shoulder, rolled, saw the line break as they raced at him. He had the Colt in hand as he rolled again to avoid a second lance. This one tore through the side of his shirt. He was cursing as the split seconds seemed like minutes and then the volley of shots exploded and he saw four of the Indians topple almost as one. Three others wheeled, let fly their arrows.

The fourth one with the armband dived from the galloping pony at him, and Fargo managed to get off one shot that missed the flying figure. He half-twisted, avoided the full force of the Indian's dive, whirled on his side as he tried to bring the Colt around again. Instead, he had to half-roll once more to avoid the tomahawk that slammed into the ground where his head had been. He heard the girls fire another volley, but it was a distant backdrop to the fury of the Indian's attack. The brave catapulted himself forward, swinging the tomahawk, and Fargo fired as he rolled, missed again, halted his rolling, and brought his two legs up to kick out with all the power of his thigh muscles. The kick caught the brave in the chest as he dived forward with the tomahawk raised, and the bronzed figure sprawled to the side, landed on his knees. Rage and reflexes brought him up instantly to spring again, but Fargo had the moment he needed. He fired from on his back, the shot hitting the Indian directly in the chest as he started to dive forward, tomahawk upraised. He seemed to hang in midair, his body shuddering, his chest suddenly caved in, and then he dropped like a stone, facedown, onto the ground. He gave a final shudder and lay still.

Fargo brought himself up on one knee, suddenly aware of the silence. His eyes swept the scene, counted seven more still, bronzed bodies, three lying only a few feet from the wagon. He rose and saw Karen's eyes searching, relief in them as she saw him. "Doris has been hit. Millie, too," she called. Fargo crossed the ground in long, loping strides, saw Chrissie and Terry pressing a torn blouse into Doris' shoulder. Millie was being administered to by Barbara and Joannie. He paused at Doris first, looked at the wound.

"Just bandage it tight," he said. "A flesh wound. It'll be all right in a few days." Millie had taken an arrow alongside the ribs, a wound more painful than serious. "You did well," he said to everyone. "Finish bandaging and move out. I want to make Beulah before our luck runs dry."

Karen rode point alongside him as they rolled west a half-hour later. "How long till we reach Beulah?" she asked.

"A day, maybe two," he guessed.

"Tonight will have to be special," she said with quiet determination.

She held to her word when she came to him in the dark of the night. He'd bedded down between two thick wild-plum shrubs. They formed a natural blanket for her cries of pure abandon as she turned the night into a frenzied quest for pleasure, bringing herself under him and on top of him, demanding he satisfy her in a thousand ways. It was as though she were trying to store up ecstasy, and perhaps she was, he reflected. But it wouldn't store, he knew. Only the memories stayed constant, feeding the hunger that returned too soon.

Before the night ended, she held his throbbing maleness, stroked and caressed it, drew her hands slowly up and down and around each vibrant side of it as if wanting to imprint it upon flesh and mind. She made her way back to the wagon that night just before the day came and the girls woke.

When they headed on that morning, the land turned

into rolling hills, mostly scrub brush with a few stands of black oak. Fargo's eyes scanned the land and he saw no homesteaders, no farm spreads, no roaming cattle let loose to forage on their own. To the west lay the Montana lands, raw and unexplored mostly; to the north the mountain men and prospectors came down from Canada; and in every direction, the Sioux and the Mandan, the Cree and the Ojibwa and the Crow. This was the upper reaches of Dakota wild and the men who came this way were mostly running away from something or after something. Yet Karen had been told the town was a settling-down place, filling with substantial settlers. Fargo frowned as he rode. The land showed no signs of it and a chill wind rolled over him as if to give emphasis to his thoughts.

The buildings came into view, and Chrissie, at the reins of the Conestoga, quickened the pace. Those riding the extra horses spurred the mounts forward to where he rode beside Karen; Fargo watched their faces as Beulah drew closer, saw the uncertain frowns, the quick exchange of glances. Karen held her face still as they neared the town, a place of rough frame buildings, dirt streets, and a few wagon barns spreading out from the main street. Fargo noted the trading post as they started down the main street, a weathered sign on an equally weathered building that read HOTEL BEULAH. A larger sign a few doors down proclaimed the town tavern and gambling house.

Karen caught his glance. "Mr. Hubbard said they'd be putting up the new school outside of town," she offered, her tone defensive. "I think we'd best stop at the hotel and ask where I can find him."

Fargo nodded agreement and drew to a halt outside the building, swung down from the pinto. The street was filled mostly with men and he saw their eyes turn to the wagon and its passengers. He saw two girls hurrying toward the dance hall, their red skirts and off-the-shoulder blouses a kind of badge. Karen dismounted and went into the hotel,

135

to return a few moments later. "Mr. Hubbard's at the dance hall and gaming house, I'm told," she said. "It seems he owns the place. The man at the desk said he owns pretty much everything here."

"Let's go see him," Fargo said. They rolled down a few hundred yards to the gaming house and this time Fargo swung down from the pinto and went inside with her. A few men were at the bar, three girls lounging at the round tables but the place mostly waited for the night trade. The bartender, a red-faced, short man, eyed Karen and then the big black-haired man beside her.

"I'm looking for Mr. Hubbard," she said.

"Wait here," the man answered, disappeared into a back room through a green drape hung over a doorless entranceway.

Thomas Hubbard came out a few minutes later and Fargo eyed the man quickly, tall enough, a round face with bright eyes, lips that edged being too thick. He wore a pin-striped suit with a touch of the dandy and his smile was expansive as he saw Karen.

"My, my, my, this is an unexpected surprise, and a delightful one," he said smoothly, beaming at Karen.

"I told you I'd be coming out with the girls," she answered.

Hubbard rubbed his hands together and his smile grew broader, more expansive. "So you did, Miss Fisher, so you did. But I didn't allow myself to hope you really meant it," he said. He was glib, Fargo commented silently, and behind the bright eyes there was a quick, darting hardness. The man took Karen's both hands in his and beamed down at her. "I can't tell you how delighted I am to see you, Miss Fisher. I take it the girls are outside?"

Karen nodded. "I didn't see anything that looked remotely like a new school," she said.

"Well, the school won't be built here in the center of

136

town. I've begun the new building a few miles west of town," the man said, still smiling warmly. His eyes flicked to Fargo, and Karen turned to the big black-haired man at her side.

"This is Skye Fargo. He got us out here," she said.

"Skye Fargo," Hubbard murmured, eyeing the big man. "Yes, I've heard that name," he said.

Fargo nodded and said nothing further.

"You really have a population here to support a girl's school and a boy's academy?" Karen asked. "Frankly, what I've seen of Beulah isn't quite what I expected."

"You've only seen the town itself," Hubbard said, beaming. "There are numerous new settlements to the north and farther west. The schools will be drawing from all those good people," he told her, his voice filling with reassurance.

Fargo's eyes moved past the man as two more men emerged through the green drape to lean against the bar, both tall, both unsmiling, hard-eyed men in cowhand outfits, both wearing .44 Walker Colts.

"Well, that's reassuring," he heard Karen say, and he grunted silently.

"Now, the first thing is to put you and your girls up until we can arrange better quarters for you. There is plenty of room upstairs here," Hubbard said.

"Here?" Karen frowned.

"No one goes upstairs, I assure you. That's quite private." Hubbard smiled, half-turned to the two men against the bar. "These are two of my men. They and the rest will make certain that you and the girls are assured of complete privacy."

"If you say so, Mr. Hubbard." Karen shrugged.

"Besides, it's all temporary. It's just that your arrival was so unexpected. I'm afraid I hadn't prepared for it," Hubbard said. He turned to the two men. "Tad, you and Jim go outside and help the young ladies in with their things. Take them in through the side door and up the stairway," he ordered. Fargo watched the two men move outside at once and Hubbard's glance went to him. "Will you be staying on, Fargo?" he asked pleasantly.

"No," Fargo said. "I'll be heading out tonight." He saw the dismay flood Karen's face at once.

"I'll be back in a few minutes," she said to Hubbard. "I want a few words alone with Fargo."

"Of course." Hubbard smiled graciously, stepped back, and Fargo followed her outside. She halted just past the door and he saw the two men taking bags and boxes from the girls.

"You don't have to just ride off like this," Karen said angrily. "You promised you'd stay for a while at least."

"I didn't promise a damn thing," he said curtly, and saw her fighting back tears. "It's best I head on. You'll be a while getting yourself settled in here and I'm not much for waiting around."

"You're rotten," she said, and he saw the hurt in her eyes.

"Sorry." He shrugged, holding back the thoughts racing through him. It wasn't time to give voice to them, not yet. She spun away, anger in her face.

"You'd best say good-bye to the girls," she said. "Or haven't you time?"

"I've time," he commented as she flung him a last reproachful glare and stalked back inside. He walked to the wagon and told them he'd be heading on. Chrissie's arms were the first to wrap around his neck and she hugged him tight.

"I don't like this place," she murmured. "I wish you were staying."

"Me neither," he heard Terry say. "It's not the way Miss Fisher told us it would be."

"It's not exactly what she thought, either," he said. "But Hubbard tells her there's a lot you haven't seen yet."

Pam kissed him after Chrissie and Terry, and Katherine was next, clinging close, then the others until they'd all had their turn. "We'll not be forgetting you, Fargo, none of us," Joannie said.

He allowed them a wide smile. "I won't be forgetting this trip, either," he said, turned quickly, and swung onto the pinto. He waved again at them and rode slowly down the street, glanced back, to see them following the two men into the side entrance. He turned and rode on, unhurriedly, and his eyes had turned blue agate. Something was wrong. He felt it inside his gut. The entire picture was out of focus and Hubbard's smooth words were too smooth, his explanations too glib. But most of all, the land gave the lie to him, and Fargo rode north and then turned west, riding easily, letting his eyes sweep the low hills. He moved back and forth across the land until the darkness began to slip over the hills. When he turned the pinto back toward the town, his jaw set tight, his eyes stayed agate. Hubbard's reassurances to Karen had been so much steer shit. There were no settlements, no clusters of new farms, only the hard, wild land and the groups of prospectors he passed.

The night lay over Beulah as he rode back into the town and halted at the dance hall. Tethering the pinto lightly, he went to the bar, ordered a bourbon. The place was crowded now, a rough, noisy, hard-drinking lot. He sipped his bourbon, waited, and after a spell Hubbard emerged through the green drape. The man's eyes traveled the room casually, halted as he saw the big black-haired man at the bar, and Fargo enjoyed the surprise in his smooth face. He saw the two cowhands appear, staying discreetly behind Hubbard. The man smiled at him as he approached.

"Fargo, how nice to see you again," he said. "Have you decided to spend some time with us here in Beulah?"

"No, my horse pulled up lame. Nothing serious, just a

sprain. I decided to rest him a bit before riding on," Fargo said. "I figure he'll be ready to ride in another hour or so."

"I hope so." The man smiled.

"Miss Fisher around?" Fargo asked casually.

"Upstairs," the man said. "But I'm afraid she's fast asleep. They're all asleep. It's been a hard trip for them."

"Sure thing," Fargo said. "Just give her my best tomorrow."

"I'll be happy to do that." Hubbard smiled. "Have your next drink on the house."

Fargo nodded thanks and the man strolled away, the two others staying close to him. Fargo finished his drink, had a second, and lingered over it. Hubbard left with his two bodyguards and Fargo's eyes went to the stairway at the side of the room. Another cowhand had taken up a position at the foot of the stairs, standing casually alert. Fargo glanced at the green-draped doorway to find a fourth man there. Hubbard was keeping his promise that Karen and the girls wouldn't be disturbed, it seemed, Fargo mused. He finished the drink and strolled out of the place, swung onto the pinto, and headed from town. He rode slowly through the night and a chill wind blew as he headed east. He'd gone not more than a quarter of a mile when he glimpsed the two riders following, staying far enough behind, and his smile was tight. He continued riding on and picked up the two men as they continued to follow, making no attempt to close ground. He took a turn across a low slope and watched the men turn with him, staying in the distance.

He kept riding, not turning to look back, taking his glimpses of the two riders following when he made a turn. As he continued riding, Fargo's jaw set in a hard line, his mouth becoming a thin slash across his face. The men followed for another hour and then he saw them peel off and head back. Someone wanted to be sure he was leaving town, someone named Hubbard. It was the final proof that the gut feeling he had inside him was more than right. Something smelled rotten and he hadn't a handle on it yet, but he had enough to know that there was no fancy school and no good solid citizens to fill one. Karen had bought a bill of goods. He turned the pinto around, took the high ground until there wasn't any more, rode slowly. He paused to let the pinto drink at a stream in the moonlight and it was deep into the predawn hours when he reached Beulah, the town asleep, the dance hall closed.

He rode along the back of the houses, keeping off the main street, and slid from the saddle as he halted opposite the darkened dance hall. On foot, he made his way along the sides of the house to the side entrance. He turned the knob slowly, his big hand enclosing it entirely, felt it open, and he grunted silently. They were too confident for their own good and he liked that. A side stairway took on shape in the dark and he tested the first step, then the second. They made no sound and he began the climb upstairs. A long kerosene lamp burned in the upstairs hallway, a dim, flickering light more than enough to see that there were none of Hubbard's men standing guard. He was at the closed door of the first room in one long stride, turned the knob slowly, and the door opened noiselessly. The room was empty and he closed the door, hurried to the next room.

Seconds later he stared into the emptiness of that room and felt the cold apprehension stabbing at him. The next room was equally empty, two beds made and unused in it. There were six rooms on the floor and they were all empty. In one, he spotted the kerchief on the floor, bent down to it, and recognized it as one Laurie had worn for most of the trip. The Trailsman's eyes were ice-blue as he straightened up, letting the kerchief remain on the floor. Hubbard's words came back to him. "They're all asleep." The cold apprehension had become bitter certainty, the

141

picture taking shape. Hubbard had plans for a girls' school, all right, but not the kind Karen had expected. Fargo pulled the door to the room closed and went back down the side stairway. Outside, he went around to the rear of the structure and saw the back entranceway. Karen and the girls had been taken somewhere and they hadn't walked. His eyes went to the ground and he knelt down, picked up the thick-rimmed unmistakable marks of the Conestoga. The tracks headed north, moving out from the rear of the dance hall. He counted the prints of horses with the wagon, at least five, maybe six or seven. They overlapped in the soft earth.

He straightened, returned to the pinto, and took off after the wagon tracks. Once they left the town, they were easy to follow, leading north up a long, slow slope and down the other side. The riders had flanked the Conestoga, he saw by the pattern of the tracks, and his eyes lifted to scan the terrain ahead. A thin line of shagbark hickory rose at the bottom of the slope and behind the trees he saw the house, a large, sprawling structure. A wide band of yellow light pushed out from the downstairs windows and Fargo moved to the trees, tethered the pinto out of sight, and crept across the few yards of open space to the house.

The largest window was open six inches from the bottom and Fargo heard the murmur of voices as he reached it, crouched low, and peered under the raised sill. He felt his muscles grow taut and his hand went to the big Colt at his side. It was with an effort that he drew it away empty. The scene seemed a painting, a brightly lighted mural too strange to be real. But it was very real, all his growing certainties given brutal, stark confirmation. Inside the large bare room, in a half-circle, the girls sat on the floor, Karen among them, all except one. Chrissie was in the center of the room, naked, hung by the wrists from a wagon-wheel chandelier piece, her toes just scraping the floor. Six men armed with carbines stood guard over the girls and, beside Chrissie, Hubbard, in shirt-sleeves, his round face looking almost benign as he looked at those on the floor. But in his right hand, Fargo saw the leather thongs of the cat-o'-nine-tails hanging down.

"Now, this is going to be an object lesson," he heard Hubbard say. "We're going to use Chrissie because she tried to escape after I told you all that couldn't be done. You've all got to see how much worse it will be to try to escape than to accept things as they're going to be. Many men will pay highly for you young lovelies. Some may even pay enough to take you off with them. I can't have you trying to run away, now, can I?"

He smiled, almost sadly, and turned to Chrissie. Fargo saw her eyes meet Hubbard's without flinching, her lithe, bubbly, young-colt body stretched out by the wrist bonds holding her arms up. Hubbard stepped back and his little smile grew broader, his thick lips drawing back as he raised the cat-o'-nine-tails. He brought the leather thongs around in a sweeping arc and Chrissie's scream split the air as the thongs drew a red slash across her waist. He struck again and she screamed again, the thongs imprinting themselves upon the tenderness of her young flesh. Her screams came with each blow and her body began to be a reddened form with thin thong lashes crossing her buttocks, her legs, her waist.

Hubbard was positioning his blows precisely and Fargo saw the thin line of perspiration on his forehead. Halting, he dropped the cat-o'-nine-tails on the floor and moved to peer at Chrissie, whose sobs came in harsh, breathy cries. He turned to the others, drew a cigar from his shirt pocket, and lighted it, let the end burn down for a moment until it was glowing. He took Chrissie by the shoulder and spun her around so that she turned freely under the wrist bonds. He let her turn for a moment, then began to jab with the burning end of the cigar, her young breasts first as they came into view and her scream of pure pain seemed to shake the room, then her nipples as she turned again. She was screaming continuously now, no words, only long, shattering shrieks. He plunged the burning cigar against the dark little triangle as she turned back again, and Chrissie wasn't the only one screaming.

Fargo heard Terry's voice over the others. "Stop, stop it, you beast," she screamed, leaped to her feet, ran at the men. One of the guards, moving quickly, brought the carbine around, the butt catching her in the stomach. She doubled over, to collapse on the floor. Karen and Katherine were on their feet, rushing at the guard, and the man swung the rifle again, using it as a club, and Fargo saw Katherine go down from a blow of the barrel and Karen topple sideways as he brought the stock around and caught her against the temple. Another guard dragged the three young women back, tossed them into the others as though they were so many sacks of potatoes.

Fargo felt the Colt in his hand, the barrel against the window frame, and he drew his lips back in a fierce grimace as he made himself pull from the trigger. He could bring Hubbard down, maybe two others, but he'd set off a wholesale shoot-out that could massacre at least half of the girls and perhaps end in his own death. He forced the gun back into the holster. It wasn't the time, not now, not yet, he told himself, and focused back on Hubbard. The man was studying Chrissie as though he were an artist examining his work. The girl had stopped screaming now, a long, low, heartrending moan coming from her. He yanked her head back by the hair, reaching up to do so, looked at her hardly conscious, pain-etched face, then let her head drop forward again.

He turned to the others, holding the cigar casually, his thick lips forming a half-smile. "That was only a sample. There are many others places I can put this," he said, waving the glowing cigar. "But I want her more conscious so we'll have another lesson tomorrow night." The thick lips suddenly drew tight and the smile vanished. "The same or more will happen to every one of you that tries running off," he barked, turned to the guards. "Take them upstairs and lock them in," he said.

Fargo watched as Pam and Joannie helped Karen to her feet, the others doing the same for Terry and Katherine. The guards herded them from the room and through an open door, up a stairway beyond. Fargo's eyes returned to Hubbard as the man drew a knife from his pocket and cut the ropes holding Chrissie's wrists. She crumpled to the floor, her whipped and scarred young body lying motionless in a heap, only the low moaning evidence that she was alive. Fargo's eyes burned into the man as he made silent promises to himself. Four of the guards returned downstairs and Hubbard turned as they came into the room. "Let's get back to town," the man said, and Fargo drew from the window. Crouching, he scuttled around to a corner of the house, kept moving to the back. He heard Hubbard and the four guards leave through the front door, mount their horses, and ride away.

The Trailsman's eyes were narrowed as he saw the thin pink edge of dawn starting to tint the sky. They had left four guards behind, and now as he began to carefully move around to the front of the house, the Colt was in his hand, his finger resting against the trigger. All but one dim lamp had been turned off in the big room downstairs and Fargo peered into the window once more. Chrissie's crumpled figure still lay on the floor and he heard the soft, broken sobs coming from it. The four guards had stayed upstairs, Fargo saw, and slowly, a fraction of an inch at a time, he began to lift the window higher. He worked carefully, soundlessly, until there was enough space for him to crawl into the room. He swung himself through the opening, landing noiselessly on the balls of

145

his feet. In two long strides he was at the naked, crumpled form, kneeling down, gently lifting her, turning her half over toward him.

She whimpered and her eyes came open, stark terror in them, and then, slowly fighting out of the daze of pain and fear, recognition came into their dark depths. He placed one hand over her lips as, wincing with pain, she lifted her arms around his neck, pressed herself against him, and he held her muffled sobs against his chest. He took his hand from her lips finally, and she put her head back, stared up at him, and in her eyes there was hope shining through the tears. Gently, he lowered her to the floor and whispered.

"Can you moan louder, Chrissie?" he asked, and she nodded.

He rose, signaled her with his eyes, and crossed the room in quick strides. He was behind the stairway in the hall outside the room as she began to moan heavily, long, harsh cries. Fargo pounded the floor with his fist as she moaned, stopped as he heard the oath from the top of the stairs. "What the hell is she doing?" he heard the voice ask harshly.

"Better go down and take a look. The boss wants her ready for more tonight," another voice said.

Fargo turned the Colt in his hand, holding it by the barrel as the footsteps came down the stairway. He glimpsed the man reach the bottom, start to turn into the room. The Trailsman moved with noiseless speed as the man stepped into the big room where Chrissie lay, crossing the hallway with one stride. He brought the heavy butt of the Colt down on the man's head with a skull-shattering thud, caught his body with his other arm before he could hit the floor, lowered him quietly. He pulled the limp figure into a corner of the room, returned to the doorway. Using his heel, he kicked hard against the wall.

"What's going on?" he heard a voice call. He kicked the wall again.

"What the hell?" the voice muttered, followed by footsteps hurrying down the stairs. Fargo was just behind the open doorway as the figure came running in. He brought the butt of the Colt around in a flat arc and heard the sound of bone shattering as the gun slammed into the point of his jaw. This time he made no effort to catch the man as he fell heavily to the floor. Instead, he stepped over the crumpled form, had the Colt ready, and was down on one knee as the two figures appeared at the top of the stairs. He fired twice, shots fired so quickly they seemed one. Neither man managed to draw his gun and Fargo rose as the two figures tumbled down the stairway, headfirst, one stopping halfway down in a grotesque tableau of twisted arms and legs, the other landing lifelessly almost at his feet. Fargo raced up the stairway, pausing to kick the other figure down to the bottom, tried the door to the first room, and found it locked. He slammed into it with his shoulder and it splintered open at once. Terry, Pam, and Joannie stared at him with disbelief, then rushed at him, clung to him, sobbing and laughing at once.

He held them for a moment, then went to the other rooms. They followed as he smashed each door open. Karen was in the last room with Millie Harris, her temple still bearing the dried blood. She fell against him, clung to him, sobbed out words. "Oh, God, I never thought you'd come back," she said. "Never, never." And she held on to him a moment longer, finally pulling away to stare up at him. "What made you come back?"

"I never figured to leave," he told her. "I just had to make you think so, and Hubbard. It didn't fit right, none of it."

"You were right all along, from the very first," Karen murmured. "I was a fool to believe him, wasn't I?"

147

"Yes," he said curtly.

"I guess I've learned a lot about deceiving oneself," she murmured.

"It's not over yet," he said. "Where's the wagon?"

"They put it alongside the other side of the house," Karen answered.

"And the rifles?"

"They took them out and put them in a storeroom."

He turned to include the others standing by. "Find the rifles and take them in the wagon with you. Chrissie's downstairs. Get some clothes for her. In time, a lot of time, she'll be all right," he said. Pam, Barbara, and Terry rushed away and he heard them running down the stairs. "When you get in the wagon, head for town and Hubbard's place," he told them, saw Karen's frown. "I'm going on ahead. I'll be waiting for you when you get there, one way or the other."

The girls started to turn away, their faces grave. Karen paused, rested her hand on his arm. "Be careful," she said. "Please don't get yourself killed."

"I don't aim to," he said. "You've got enough on your conscience."

Her eyes looked away and she hurried on after the others, her head lowered. Fargo waited, reloaded the Colt, and heard the girls outside with the wagon. He made his way down the stairs, broke into an easy lope until he reached the line of trees where he'd left the pinto. He turned the horse toward Beulah and rode at an easy canter in the light of the new day. The town hadn't come awake yet as he reached the edge of it; he headed the pinto behind the buildings until he neared the silent dance hall. He dismounted, took the lariat from the saddle horn, and went the rest of the way on foot. Through an alleyway, he saw the two men on guard in front of the structure, the two hard-faced ones who acted as Hubbard's personal bodyguards. They expected no trouble. One

148

lounged against the post holding the overhang of the roof, the other sat on the step outside the door. Fargo moved on the balls of his feet, silent as a mountain lion, the lariat in one hand, circled to the back of the structure. Draping the rope on one arm, he found a foothold alongside the tin drainpipe, pulled himself up to the second level, rested, let the muscles in his arms gather strength again. Drawing his breath in deeply, he went on, pulling himself along the uneven yet smooth edges of the drainpipe until his fingers seemed as though they'd lock in place.

He reached the roofline and used his forearms to lift himself over; he lay flat and let his breath return. Slowly, he flexed his fingers until the strained muscles loosened and circulation returned to the digits. He made fists, then unclenched his hands, satisfied the speed and sensitivity had returned to them. He rose to a crouch, moved catlike across the roof till he was at the front of the structure. He uncoiled the lariat, drew the double-edged throwing knife from inside his boot. Below, the two men hadn't changed positions and he took a step closer to the edge of the overhang. It had to be done with split-second timing and in silence. He loosened the lariat, formed the noose, draped the rope over his left arm. He chose the one standing first, raised the throwing knife, and sent it hurtling through the air, as swift and accurate as the strike of a hawk.

The blade struck the man in the back of the neck, the tip of it coming out the other side of his throat. His hands grabbed at his neck as he pitched forward to the ground. The second one was just leaping to his feet in surprise when the lariat whistled through the air. He was reaching for his holster as the noose snapped around his neck and Fargo pulled. The man's head snapped sideways, his mouth falling open soundlessly, and Fargo yanked hard on the lariat and the man's feet left the ground. Fargo

149

pulled slowly, the already lifeless figure rising upward, twirling at a thirty-degree angle as he reached the edge of the overhang. Fargo pulled him over the edge and rolled him onto the flat part of the roof, took the lariat from him, and fastened one end to the corner roof-support beam. He swung himself over the roof, holding the other end of the lariat, and lowered himself to the ground.

He opened the door to the dance hall a fraction of an inch, enough to peer inside, the new day pushing the dimness away as the light came through the window. The downstairs was empty and Fargo turned away for a moment, retrieved his knife, wiped it clean on the dead man's shirt, and slipped inside the dance hall. They had all been willing partners in Chrissie's torture. They had paid the price for it, but Hubbard was the mastermind, the one who'd enjoyed it most. He was owed payment not only by Chrissie but by all of them. Fargo moved across the floor of the room, skirting the empty tables, moved along the edge of the bar toward the green-draped doorway. He paused at the drape, the Colt in his hand, let his fingers coil around the edge of the material. He flung it aside and plunged through the doorway in one motion. The two guards were a dozen feet away, down a hallway longer than he'd guessed, flanking a closed door. Both men whirled in surprise, hands flying toward their holsters. Fargo's shot caught the nearest one in the chest and the man went backward hard against the wall. The second one managed to get his gun out when Fargo's shot pierced him directly through the heart. He slumped backward and fell half against the wall, the gun still clutched in his hand.

"What the hell?" he heard Hubbard shout from inside the room, and stepped back as the door flew open and the man appeared in trousers only, a small gambler's pistol in one hand, a double-barrel European gun. Hubbard's eyes went to the two figures outside the door, then to the big black-haired man in the doorway.

"Drop the gun," Fargo growled, and the man opened his hand, let the gun fall from his fingers. He had a thin layer of fat covering a square, chunky body and the darting eyes were small and vicious now.

"I underestimated you," the man said. "Badly, I'm afraid."

"This way," Fargo said, backing out of the doorway into the main room. Hubbard followed, his eyes flicking to the gun and back to Fargo's face.

"Go on, shoot," the man said. "I'm not going to try rushing you."

"No, not just like that," Fargo growled. "That'd be too easy for you." He saw Hubbard's eyes grow narrow, wary. Fargo motioned with the gun and the man moved to stand beside one of the tables as Fargo went behind the bar. Keeping the Colt trained on his half-naked quarry, he took a bottle of whiskey, flung it over the bar and onto the floor where it shattered at once. He sent another after it, followed it with a third until the floor was littered with pieces of broken bottle. He came around the bar, took the Colt, and placed it atop the smooth wood of the long bar and sent it spinning to the far end. His lake-blue eyes were agate flame as he stared at Hubbard.

"Now's your chance, you sadistic, rotten bastard," Fargo said. "Take me and you'll get away."

The man's eyes darted to the gun at the far end of the bar and Fargo motioned with his hands. Hubbard's mouth curled in an instant's smile, turned into a thick, harsh line. He started slowly toward the big black-haired man, his thick body pulling itself into a half-crouch. Fargo's arms hung loosely, waiting to strike when Hubbard half-spun, seized hold of a stout wooden chair beside the table. Using it as a ramrod, he flung himself at the Trailsman, moving with surprising speed. Fargo raised his arms protectively, but the legs of the chair caught him in the chest, drove him back against the bar. Hubbard pulled back, swung with the chair, and Fargo had to duck. As the chair whistled over his head, he sank a curving right into Hubbard's midsection.

"That's for Laurie," he said as Hubbard's breath rushed from him in a hard, wheezing sound. Fargo followed with an arcing blow that landed on the side of the man's jaw, and Hubbard flew back to crash into one of the tables. "That's for Karen," Fargo rasped. Hubbard, on one knee, dived forward, tackling Fargo around the knees with surprising force, and Fargo felt himself go backward and down on one knee. Hubbard tried to bring a short uppercut to the jaw, but Fargo, instead of ducking back, moved in and the blow struck him in the chest. He brought his own fist downward, catching the man behind the ear. "That's for Terry," he said as Hubbard went down on all fours. The man grabbed at Fargo's legs again, but the Trailsman twisted out of his grip, reached down, seized the man's bare torso with both hands, lifted, and using all the power of his shoulder muscles, Fargo flung Hubbard into the air. The man landed on the floor covered with broken glass and his scream filled the air.

"Oooowwwoooo . . . oh, Jesus," he cried out, stumbled to his feet, and his bare torso was bleeding in half-a-dozen places.

"That's for Chrissie," Fargo said, moving forward quickly, lashing out with a right aimed at the man's temple, carrying just enough force to knock him down again, this time on his back.

"Aaagggghhhh!" Hubbard screamed, half-rolled, cried out again, and now he was running blood from all over his back and shoulders.

"For Chrissie," Fargo hissed, stepped in quickly as Hubbard tried to duck away from another blow and wasn't fast enough as Fargo's fist slammed into the middle

152

of his back as though it were a sledgehammer. Hubbard went down, his face sprawling onto the floor and his guttural cry sent spurts of blood cascading. He raised his head, screamed from torn and bloodied lips. "For Chrissie, everything for Chrissie, you bastard," Fargo growled through tight lips, smashed the man's face down on the floor again, then yanked him up. Fargo looked down at a face that was torn and slashed, bleeding from a dozen places, shreds of skin hanging loose.

"No more, oh, Christ, no more," Hubbard pleaded.

"I'll listen the way you listened to Chrissie," Fargo said, sank a blow into the man's blood-smeared abdomen, and Hubbard dropped to his knees, gasped out a half-scream as his kneecaps spurted red. Fargo flung him on his back and again the man screamed, a gargled, guttural sound now. His body was a thing of dripping blood, dozens and dozens of jagged cuts made of torn, ripped flesh, his face hardly visible, blood coursing down from every part of the torn skin. Fargo took him by the belt with one hand, his hair by the other, lifted him, and flung him over the bar, heard the thudding crash of his body on the other side and the deep groaning that followed.

He kicked glass from underfoot as he strode to the far end of the bar, picked up the Colt, and put it into its holster. He started for the front door, his jaw tight, not looking back. He'd almost reached it when the rifle blast exploded. He flung himself to one side automatically, hit the floor, and turned, the Colt in his hand. He saw Chrissie, standing by the side door, the rifle in her hand and his eyes spun to the bar. Hubbard, a shotgun in his bloody hands, was just falling backward, his head now obliterated completely.

Fargo, at Chrissie's side in one long stride, gently took the rifle from her. She leaned against him and he held her for a long moment. "Thanks," he murmured. "I should've figured there might be a rifle under the bar. I owe you."

She looked at him, her eyes still wide, unsmiling. "No, I wouldn't be here if it weren't for you, Fargo," she said.

The front door flew open and he saw the others rushing in, Karen first, Terry and Pam with Spencers in their hands.

"She jumped from the wagon and rushed in the side door," Karen said of Chrissie.

"It's done now, the score settled," Fargo said, and stepped back as Laurie and Joannie came to take Chrissie away between them. The others drifted outside, following, and Karen stayed to walk beside him as he stepped into the bright morning sun. A crowd had gathered outside, watching silently. No one said anything as the girls climbed into the wagon and Fargo, on the pinto, Karen on the bay beside him, led the way out of Beulah. He rode slowly, stopped by a stream for fresh water, went on until the day neared an end, and found a spot to camp for the night. Each young face wore exhaustion and strain, and the night was hardly an hour old when they were asleep. Karen came to where he'd stretched his bedroll, knelt down beside him, and the strain was in her face, too, making the delicate lines deep, her eyes shadowed.

"What do you figure to do?" he asked her.

"Make it back east if we can," she said, and voiced the question in her eyes. "Can we? If we pick up the other wagon?"

He grunted grimly. "We were lucky once. I wouldn't like to count on it twice," he said.

She shrugged helplessly. "I have to try. There's no other choice," she said.

"You're right this time," he agreed, and she buried her face against him. He lay down, drew her into his arms, and held her until she slept. It wasn't a night for making love. It was a night for holding until the taste of the day grew less bitter. He watched the stars and wondered if he

154

had enough luck still on credit. Just a little, he murmured silently, not for himself. He slept soon, soundly, until the dawn came and he was up first, scanning the horizon. There was nothing to do but try. Karen had been right on that and it was a silent troupe that set out again. Another few days and they'd be starting to cross the prairie again and Fargo's jaw grew tight at the thought.

But Lady Luck could smile. Hell, he'd seen that often enough in poker games and now he saw it in the fast-moving cloud of dust on the horizon. He rode on alone to investigate and his smile pulled slowly at the corners of his mouth as he saw the red-and-yellow regimental flags catch the sun. He sent the pinto into a gallop and crossed the path of the full regiment of horse soldiers, a captain and a lieutenant leading the troop. They reined to a halt as he swung in front of them.

"Mister, that's too wild a story for any man to make up," the captain said when he'd finished.

"It is that," Fargo agreed. "I'll show you proof of it if you'll follow me."

"Lead the way," the captain said, and Fargo turned the pinto around.

"I didn't think the Army had a full troop out this far in the Dakota Territory," he said.

"It doesn't. We were on a special reconnaissance mission checking out the number of Sioux," he said.

"What'd you find?" Fargo asked.

"More than we wanted. I'll be glad to get out of here," the captain said.

Fargo met the Conestoga halfway back and saw the astonishment on the part of the officers and the rest of the troop. He introduced them to Karen, and the captain pushed his cap back as he surveyed the cargo in the Conestoga. "We're not heading east but we are going to St. Cloud in Minnesota Territory. A proper caravan can take you back east from our post there," he said.

155

"I'd be much obliged," Fargo said.

"That goes for all of us," Karen echoed.

"We were going to make camp another ten miles on and rest the night," the captain said. "But we'll make good time tomorrow."

"That's fine with me," Karen said, flashing a glance at Fargo. As the troopers broke ranks to flank the wagon, she took him aside. "One last night, Fargo. I'll need it. I can live on the memory."

"You ought to have enough memories now," he said.

"No, not of you. Please," she said, and he nodded, turned away, and climbed onto the pinto. He rode back of the troopers and made his own camp away from the main one.

The moon hung high when Karen came to him. She pressed her mouth to his without words, drew him to her, and made the night one she'd remember for always. He'd not forget it either, he admitted, and she paused as she rose to leave before the dawn came.

"I told the girls I was coming to you," she said.

"Confession is good for the soul," Fargo commented. "They say anything?"

"Hooray for me," she said. "What are you going to do now?" she asked.

He shrugged. "Head into north country," he said. "Montana way. Look up an old friend."

She turned, walked away, not looking back, and he understood. It wasn't until he lay down again that he found the neat little packet wrapped in paper at the edge of the bedroll. He opened it, counted twelve hundred dollars. He was glad he had earned every hundred of it. He saddled the pinto in the first day's light and took the trail northwest into the new sun.

*Montana, 1861, not yet a territory,
at the edge of the High Plains country
where the Rocky Mountains rise
in wild and terrible splendor.*

## 1

The old man lay on the floor of the little cabin, facedown,
as if he'd dozed off to sleep. But his body held at least six
bullet holes and the big black-haired man bent over the
lifeless form. Gently, Fargo turned the old man over,
studied the worn face, a cap of short, white hair atop it, a
good face, nothing small or mean in it. But the old man
lay dead, an old man alone in his cabin gunned down sav-
agely. Fargo frowned into space for a moment as he knelt
beside the body. He had heard the shots while he was still
a ways off, had spurred his horse on until he came in
sight of the cabin as he topped the ridge.

He'd halted then, waited, watched, looked down at the

cabin, and when nothing stirred except the smoke from
the chimney, the coldness had grabbed at him inside. He
had circled carefully, moving down to the cabin, his eyes
scanning the surrounding terrain. Drawing up to the
cabin, he had called out and the coldness inside him grew;
there was no answer, but the door hung open. He'd seen
the figure the moment he stepped into the cabin, and now
he lifted his head at the soft sound behind him at the
doorway. He turned, reaching for his gun, had time only
to glimpse the girl in the doorway, long, black hair fram-
ing a pretty face that was contorted in anguish. He
glimpsed the big Henry carbine in her hands just as she
fired, a half-cry tearing from her at the same instant. He
tried to twist away, but the blast caught him alongside the
temple. The figure of the girl faded away, the world became red and purple, and then nothing as he fell sideways
through endless space.

  He didn't see the girl fling herself beside the figure of
the old man, cradle the worn head in her arms, and he
didn't hear the sobs that tore from her as she rocked back
and forth holding the lifeless form. He didn't see or hear,
but he knew he was alive. The emptiness began to throb,
pain entering the void, and only the living feel pain. He
felt his eyelids move, flutter, his eyes blink. The world
was still purple and it became gray and through the
grayness, form, shape, outlines. He blinked again, managed to make out ceiling beams, and the world began to
take on meaning. The side of his temple was sticky and it
hurt. He began to pull himself up on one elbow, tried to
focus, and with maddening slowness, memory began to
push itself forward. He blinked his eyes and the girl
slowly came into focus, all blurred first, then taking on
definition.

  Her voice was a sharp whip to the senses and his head
cleared and he saw her sharply, standing before him, the
big carbine pointed at him. The old man lay at her feet,

he saw. "You're alive, you stinking, rotten bastard," she spit at him. "I'm glad. You don't deserve to die that quick."

Fargo's lake-blue eyes saw the tear-stained cheeks, the reddened eyes, and the edge-of-hysterics anguish in her face. "Get up, goddamn you, get up," she exploded, screaming the words. He rose slowly, the pain of his temple now more annoying than serious. She'd fired the blast in fury and haste and he'd been lucky for that. "Drop the gun belt," she screamed. "Easy or I'll blast you in half."

"Now, hold on, girlie," Fargo tried.

*"Drop it!"* she screamed, and he saw her finger tighten on the trigger of the carbine. He undid the gun belt, let it fall to the floor. She was on the edge of doing anything. "Kick it over here," she ordered, and he obeyed.

"You're making a mistake," he began again.

"Goddamn bushwhacking, murdering bastard," she flung at him. "Drop those pants."

"Listen to me," he tried.

"Drop them," she exploded, and he saw her tremble in fury. "I'm going to shoot your goddamn balls off and I don't want to miss," she barked.

"I didn't kill the old man," Fargo said.

"Goddamn liar," she flung back. "Drop the pants."

Her breath came wrapped harshly around her sentences and Fargo saw the pain and the fury in her eyes, deep, black-brown eyes. He kept his voice calm. She was no killer. Rage and fury drove her. He had to try to reach her. "Just go on and shoot me," he said. "Go on."

"No, too good for you," she hissed. "After I shoot your balls off, I'm going to blast your kneecaps into bits, just in case they don't hang you." She raised the carbine, took aim. "The pants, goddamn you."

Fargo put one hand on his belt buckle, started to loosen it. He swayed, let his eyes half-close, took a half-step, and raised one hand toward his temple. He swayed again and collapsed, sinking to the floor, his body gone limp. "Damn," he heard her say, saw her through eyes opened but a fraction, caught the movement of the rifle as she lowered it. His body lashed forward with the speed of a snake, his hand seizing the barrel of the rifle, forcing it down. She gasped and fired, but the bullet went into the floor, and then he twisted, flinging her sideways as he ripped the carbine from her hands. He flung it aside and went after her as she fell to one knee. Her hands came up clawing, and he narrowly avoided being raked across the face, barreled into her, and sent her sprawling on the cabin floor. He fell half over her, pinned her arms back against the floor.

"I'll kill you," she screamed. "Goddamn murdering bastard, I'll kill you." She tried to get a knee up, but he knocked her leg aside with his thigh, drew his hand back, and slapped her across the face. "Owooo!" she gasped, and her head thudded against the floor.

"I didn't kill him, dammit," he said, banged her head on the floor again, not as hard this time. She glared up at him, rage still burning in her eyes. He repeated the words again, slowly giving each one emphasis. "I didn't kill him."

"Liar," she spit out. "There was nobody else. I didn't pass anyone."

"Neither did I. But there was somebody else. I didn't do it," Fargo said. She continued to stare up at him, rage and pain still holding her, filling her with unwillingness to trust anything or anyone. "I'll prove it," he said.

"You can't prove it," she snapped.

He let go of her, pushed himself to his feet, and yanked her up with him. He reached down with one hand, swept the carbine up, and pushed it at her.

"Take it," he said. "I didn't do, I tell you. Take it back."

She looked at the rifle, her eyes moving back to his, and he saw the flicker of uncertainty suddenly coloring the fury. She reached out for the rifle tentatively and he pushed it at her again. "Go on, take it," he said. She closed her hand around it and he saw her tense, waiting for him to pull it back. He didn't move, let it pass to her. She swung the barrel at him, but now there was only confusion and pain in her eyes and he kept his stare hard on her. She let the barrel hang downward and her eyes went past him to the old man on the floor. Slowly, she sank down on the floor, soft sobs escaping her lips.

Fargo watched her, took her in fully for the first time. Her jet hair framed a face with deep, wide-set eyes, a classic aquiline nose, fine-lined eyebrows. It was a face that normally carried determination, perhaps a touch of arrogance, he was certain. She wore a white cotton blouse that set loosely over full breasts that filled the garment beautifully, riding jeans over legs that seemed long and well-turned. His eyes went to her face again, cream skin stained by tears, her lips full and generous, a face not quite beautiful but a lot more than pretty.

Her eyes lifted to him and the surge of uncertainty pushed into their black depths. "Maybe you're just a slick one," she muttered, glowering at him, her hand tightening around the carbine.

"Come outside with me," he said. "You've got the gun." He started for the door and she followed, staying far enough behind him. He went to where the Ovaro waited, the magnificent horse standing quietly, let his eyes go to her mount, a good chestnut with fast lines. The ground showed no other prints and he began to walk around the cabin as she followed. At the rear of the little cabin he halted, dropped to one knee, gestured to the ground. She came closer and he put his hands on the hoofprints nearest.

"Three, I make it," he said, sweeping out with his hand

to take in the other prints. She stared at the prints and he peered more closely at one set. "One horse wears an extra-size shoe," he said. He got to his feet and his eyes went to the distant rise. "They cut out straight over that crest," he said, and his eyes stayed on the horizon where the first great tower of land rose into the air, the citadels of the untamed land they called the Rocky Mountains, cutting across the land, the vast and fierce wildness the Crow called the Killing Mountains. In the Rocky Mountains, only the very strong, the very lucky, or the very wild survived.

These mountains seemed to touch the sky, rose beyond the first towering peak in row upon row, lush and green at the bottom, growing browner as they rose, and at the very top, where few men had ever been and lived to tell of it, the caps of whiteness, ice and snow that never changed. The trees were just beginning to take on color, Fargo noted. Soon they would be a riot of brilliance, flame-red and yellow, rust and orange, a crazy quilt of color laid over the mountainsides. And something more. A terrible warning encased in a glorious beauty.

He brought his eyes back to the girl. She was still staring at the tracks. "That's why you didn't see anyone and neither did I. They cut straight up. And fast, too. See how those hoofprints are dug deep?"

She turned her eyes to him and there was only pain there now. "I'm sorry. I guess I went a little crazy," she said.

Fargo returned to the cabin and she followed. "Who was he?" he asked as she slumped down on the edge of a frame cot.

"A friend," she said simply. "Someone I've talked to ever since I was a little girl. Someone who never hurt anyone or anything." Her voice took on fury at once. "Why? Why, dammit? Why did they kill him?"

Fargo's glance went around the little cabin and he

shrugged. "Can't say. Can't see anything taken or anything worth taking."

The girl rose, went to a large jar in the corner of the room. She opened the lid and peered in. "He kept his money in here, what there was of it," she said. "It's still there."

"Maybe he wouldn't tell them where it was," Fargo said.

She shook her head. "He'd have told them. He didn't believe in being a damnfool. He loved life too much."

"But they killed him," Fargo said, letting his lips purse. It didn't make sense, an old man alone out here, killing and not taking anything. No sense at all to it, and most killings had some kind of sense, warped and strange as it might be. "He had a name," Fargo said quietly.

"John Enders," she said.

"How about you?" he asked.

"Melody," she said. "Melody Adams." She held his eyes, waited.

"Fargo," he told her. "Skye Fargo." She nodded and he gazed out the open door. "He have any other friends besides you?"

"The Wilsons, Sam, Harriet, and their boy, Tad," she said. "They live just a mile or so from here. Sam raises goats, sells the milk, too."

"Maybe you'd best tell them," Fargo said. "You can get somebody back here later to tend to what has to be done."

She nodded, her face unsmiling. "Will you come with me?" she asked. "Please. I'm really pretty shaky."

"Why not?" he said. He'd been just passing through. A few hours' delay would mean little.

"Wait," she said as he started to turn away. He stopped and she went to the iron kettle by the fireplace, came back with a kerchief wet. She washed the dried blood from his temple, her touch gentle, patted him dry. He saw her swallow hard, her eyes grow rounder. "Oh, God, I'm sorry. What if I'd killed you? My God," she gasped.

"You didn't," he said.

"I'm glad you duck fast," she breathed.

"I'm glad you shoot too fast," he said, and strode from the cabin. She swung onto the chestnut and rode alongside him, pointing the way across a rolling hillside. She rode well, he saw, her jet hair flying out behind her and the white shirt pressing tight against the full breasts. Her face, from the side, had strong yet delicate planes and the touch of arrogance was there again. "The Wilsons, they know him as long as you?" Fargo asked as they rode.

"Longer," she said. "They were old friends before they came out here." She led the way over the top of the hill, down the other side, and then along a small incline until they came in sight of a modest house with two outbuildings. Fargo saw the herd of goats corralled by the outbuildings. A full feed bucket rested on the ground halfway between the house and the corral. Melody started to send the chestnut down the incline when he halted her, pulling the reins back on her. She frowned at once at him, saw his eyes were steady on the house below.

He waited, letting his eyes travel back and forth across the house and the outbuildings. The door of the house hung open and his eyes returned to the full feed bucket on the ground. He waited further. No one appeared in the doorway of the house. No one came from the outbuildings. The goats bleated and in between there was only silence and the full feed bucket rested untouched. Fargo felt the coldness curling inside him again.

## MENTOR, SIGNET and SIGNET CLASSIC Books of Special Interest

☐ **THE WESTERN WRITINGS OF STEPHEN CRANE edited and with an Introduction by Frank Bergon.** This unique collection brings together Crane's experiences when he went west for the first time in 1895. His perceptive writing skillfully depicts drought-parched Nebraska, the brawling city of Galveston, and cowboys living on their legends in New York —everything the West meant and still means today.
(#CJ1189—$1.95)

☐ **LOOKING FAR WEST: The Search for the American West in History, Myth, and Literature edited by Frank Bergon and Zeese Papanikolas.** Here in song and story, myth and first-hand report, analysis and eulogy, is an anthology that gives full expression to the West in all its complex meanings. With 16 pages of photographs. (#ME1645—$2.50)

☐ **CROW KILLER by Raymond W. Thorp and Robert Bunker.** The monumental true saga of the greatest Mountain Man of the West, who swore revenge on an entire Indian nation. "It merits study by those who sense the raw, brutal approach that shoved the frontier from tidewater to tidewater."—*San Francisco Chronicle* (#W9366—$1.50)

☐ **THE OREGON TRAIL by Francis Parkman.** Foreword by A. B. Guthrie, Jr. A true narrative of the dangers and excitements encountered by a group of American explorers in the old West. (#CE1377—$1.75)

---

Great Reading from SIGNET

## Big Bestsellers from SIGNET

- [ ] **THE DEAD ZONE by Stephen King.** (#E9338—$3.50)
- [ ] **'SALEM'S LOT by Stephen King.** (#E9827—$3.50)
- [ ] **THE STAND by Stephen King.** (#E9828—$3.95)
- [ ] **THE SHINING by Stephen King.** (#E9216—$2.95)
- [ ] **CARRIE by Stephen King.** (#E9544—$2.50)
- [ ] **SPHINX by Robin Cook.** (#E9745—$2.95)
- [ ] **COMA by Robin Cook.** (#E9756—$2.75)
- [ ] **BLOOD RITES by Barry Nazarian.** (#E9203—$2.25)*
- [ ] **THE NIGHTTIME GUY by Tony Kenrick.** (#E9111—$2.75)*
- [ ] **THE SCOURGE by Nick Sharman.** (#E9114—$2.25)*
- [ ] **THE SURROGATE by Nick Sharman.** (#E9293—$2.50)*
- [ ] **INTENSIVE FEAR by Nick Christian.** (#E9341—$2.25)*
- [ ] **THE DEATH MECHANIC by A. D. Hutter.** (#J9410—$1.95)*
- [ ] **TRANSPLANT by Len Goldberg.** (#J9412—$1.95)
- [ ] **JOGGER'S MOON by Jon Messmann.** (#J9116—$1.95)*
- [ ] **LABYRINTH by Eric MacKenzie-Lamb.** (#E9062—$2.25)*

*Price slightly higher in Canada

Buy them at your local
bookstore or use the coupon
on page 165 for ordering.